RESTING WITCH FACE

A WIDOW'S BAY NOVEL

REBECCA REGNIER

CHAPTER 1

"*I* changed the intro, Wyatt. You might want to let him know."

"I've got to check on the cold open editing. Can you do it?" Wyatt asked. He was running at top speed in the final moments before airtime.

"Yeah, no problem."

Wyatt Douglas produced the six-o'clock news. Sam and I were the husband and wife anchor team for WXYD's six o'clock newscast.

Sam was the face -- handsome, charming -- and I was the storyteller. It was a perfect on-air match. We'd been number one in the ratings for a decade.

"You know he'll just read the box, right?" The box was the teleprompter. Sam could translate the words in the box into warmth, truth, concern, alarm, whatever the story required.

Ad-libbing? Not so much.

That was my favorite, going off the cuff and rolling with changes.

The truth was our talents were complimentary. Even if I was annoyed at how little Sam cared about the stories some days when the red light turned on, there was no question that, as an anchorman, Sam crushed it.

I always got out to the set and in place way ahead of Sam, getting my hair right, my undereye concealer applied, and my microphone positioned, all of which took longer and longer the older I got. The more I worked to look "perfect" the less it lasted. Makeup disappeared into my wrinkles, never to be seen again. Exfoliating, something my skin did on its own in my youth, now required time blocked out in my day planner.

I was usually on set a good ten minutes ahead of news time these days to be sure a gray hair hadn't sprouted and escaped confinement. I decided I'd quickly pop into Sam's office on the way to my anchor chair. He sucked when it came to script changes on the fly, so I'd let him know the introduction to my story on new jobs coming to the Upper Peninsula was slightly different. He hated being caught off guard.

His door was closed, but I wasn't an intern, or a producer, or giving a station tour. I was his wife and colleague of almost twenty years.

And I was also a complete idiot.

I swung open the door.

"Sam, I changed the intro just a bit, and…"

"You're supposed to be on set!" Sam's eyes flew open in surprise, and he took a step back.

There was a human person attached to the mid-section of my husband.

Kayleigh Carson, the newest reporter at the station, was at Sam's feet. Looking less than surprised and not embarrassed in the slightest by my surprise entrance.

It took a second or two to register what I had walked in on.

My handsome husband, co-anchor, and father of my children was exactly who I'd feared he might be.

"Sam, be careful not to mess up her lipstick. Her story airs right after mine. Also, double-check the lead. I made some changes."

I spun on my heel and slammed his office door, then walked back to the set.

My face was hot, my heart raced, and I was having a hard time swallowing. When I did swallow, it felt like acid in my stomach.

I walked up on the platform. The plexiglass anchor desk was lit and ready for the newscast. The glowing red and blue screens surrounded me.

I sat in the anchor chair, patted my face with powder, and did all the pre-show rituals I performed every day. I pulled it together.

The previous few seconds changed the memories that played in my head of the last few years. We'd raised the twins, built careers, and lived a picture-perfect life, one that looked great in our anchor bios.

But it was like some filter over my life had been removed. The varnish we'd applied to everything seared off in seconds.

Now that the boys were college men, Sam felt no real need to keep it in his pants.

Ugh.

And yes, I knew he flirted with, well, everyone. That was part of his charm; he was charismatic, and he backed it up with great hair. Everyone liked a charismatic person. I told myself the flirting meant nothing.

Except it did.

Primal anger edged out the initial shock of my current situation.

To do this at work, my work, his work, was a special kind of selfish.

I started doing mental calculations, adding up the inconsistencies that I'd never paid attention to before. I wasn't a suspicious person. I didn't care where he went or what he did. I had my own life; I had the kids. If he was late to an appointment, I brushed it off. If a text seemed suspicious, it was spam. Suddenly things I hadn't paid attention to were neon signals that someone else was paying attention.

In those moments, the memory files of my brain were being rewritten. My marriage was now my marriage 2.0. And it sure as heck wasn't an upgrade.

"You okay?" I was startled back to the present by Wyatt's voice in my ear as he stood in the booth with me.

"Yeah. Sam's on the way."

"He knows about the intro change?"

"Yes, yes, he does." That was true. I did tell him.

I took a deep breath.

I had anchored newscasts while pregnant, while sick, while sad, while tired, while pissed off, and I'd done it all with a focus that I was proud of. I was going to get through this one too.

Sam walked in and sat next to me. He clipped on his mic and then put his hand over it to shield it, so no one would hear him but me.

"I want a divorce," he said.

I was expecting an apology, maybe a little shame from the man. I got neither.

Kayleigh walked into the studio, looking young, beautiful, and I think victorious. She stood at the big monitor, ready to introduce her story.

I didn't say anything to Sam, or Kayleigh, or Wyatt.

The show opening music played, and we were live on the air.

"You're watching WXYD Action News at six, with Sam Barkley and Marzie Nowak." I'd kept my name. That seemed very Tina Turner of me about now.

"Good evening. Tonight, we bring you breaking developments on possible new jobs headed for the state." The camera shot showed us side by side as Sam delivered the lead lines perfectly. Smooth was his middle name.

It was my turn to take over. As we did every night, I said one sentence, and Sam looked over to me like it was a conversation at the dinner table. A dinner table with the city skyline behind us, but that was our shtick; viewers were watching a husband and wife tell you about the news of the day.

"That is if the Chippewa County Commissioners can agree," I said the line I'd written for myself, and Sam nodded to indicate that yes indeedy, that was a fact.

The camera turned to a single shot of just me and the teleprompter. Sam was still next to me, and Kayleigh was smiling at the corner of the set. But on televisions and cell phones across Lower Michigan, all people saw was me, head, and shoulders. Meltdown in three, two, one…

I hadn't planned it. I thought I was going to deliver the news as usual and deal with Sam and Kayleigh afterward.

Instead, I snapped. I Z-snapped. I snapped like a front bra clasp on prom night. I snapped like my Spanx after Thanksgiving Dinner. It was a full and complete snapping.

And it was all live on the air.

"Sam and I have been married for almost twenty years, and have been so honored in that time, to bring you the news. A lot of you didn't know that I met Sam when I was just a young intern, and he was a reporter here. Romantic right? Or maybe it's creepy? Ha. You be the judge. I got pregnant, and we got married, and you've watched our twins Joe and Sam Junior grow up. Now they're at college and Sam keeps getting younger-looking, doesn't he? That's the deal for men, right? Men look better and better as they age, and women need more and more moisturizer!"

"MARZIE, what the hell are you doing?" Wyatt was yelling at me in my ear. I ignored it. Sam sat there, oddly, with a smile, and nodded. It was what he was trained to do.

I barreled ahead.

"I just wanted to take a moment to let you know that Sam Barkley is a complete and total ass. So much so that he didn't bother to have his affairs at hotels. Nope, he had one right here at the station, under my nose. After almost twenty years of marriage, I walked in and found my husband and..." My voice was at a low yell at this moment in my monologue.

At that point, the station cut to commercial.

"What the hell are you doing?" Sam hissed at me. I heard footsteps running toward the studio.

"Giving the viewers the facts! That's my job!" I was at screech audio level now.

Sam and Kayleigh had the guts to do whatever they wanted wherever they wanted. I had always been so careful about everything -- ethics, appearances, even manners.

All of my restraint vanished, and in its place, I unleashed a tirade decades in the making. I envisioned terrible things and hoped they were visited upon my cheating husband. His handsome face looked distorted and ugly to me now. I used to see my sons in his eyes, and now I hoped my sons would never see him the way I did. Because it was ugly.

"Roll a PSA!" I heard the news director yell in the control room.

"You're acting like a child," Sam said to me.

"I thought that's what you liked since you're having an affair with one!"

"I'm 23," Kayleigh said, and I whirled around to look at her. The force of my glare had physical power, or it seemed to because the pretty blonde who'd been helping Sam with his fly moments before the newscast staggered backward into the monitor. My anger pushed her off her feet.

I didn't care about her, though. I had been her. I cared that my husband had just made a proper fool of me and had probably been doing it for years.

"Sam, here's my concealer. It looks like something nasty is erupting there, on your lip."

I threw my entire makeup bag at Sam. Brushes, powders and

lipsticks ricocheted off his perfect chin and his swoosh of meticulously groomed blonde hair.

The news director, Tad Gray, our boss, arrived in the studio as the powder wafted into the air.

Managers converged on me, but they approached slowly. I was a grenade with the pin already pulled out.

"Yeah, I get it. I'm out." I ripped the mic off my tastefully tailored blazer and walked off set.

No one followed me.

I looked at a television monitor as I walked out of the station. Sam did, in fact, have a giant boil developing on his upper lip. The ugly inside of him struggled to make itself real on the outside. That's all I could think. Though I knew, deep down, that my anger had just manifested itself on Sam and that Kayleigh.

I pushed aside what I'd feared lately, about myself. Bottom line, Sam, and Kayleigh were wrong, and I was righteous

Sam read his anchor script into the camera and, he appeared unshaken. The newscast went on without me.

My marriage and my career were now a raging dumpster fire.

Within an hour of me coming apart on television, someone uploaded the clip of me losing it onto the internet.

Anchorwoman goes ballistic live on the air...

The headline wasn't wrong.

It only took a few hours to go viral.

Twenty years of local news, and I was finally a national sensation.

And fired.

SAM GOT THE HOUSE, and he kept the anchor chair.

I got a buyout package from the station.

It wasn't hard to predict that outcome. Viewers loved Sam. They wanted to have a beer with him. I was shrill. That's what the research from the consultants revealed over the last few years. I was always being told to smile more. I resisted the light stories and went for the crime or investigative pieces.

Sam was their handsome friend. I was their nagging wife. Softening my presentation was always the goal of the TV news experts.

One epic television meltdown, and I was packing my bags and signing divorce papers. Sam was the cheater, but who could blame him, right? Ugh.

On the flip side, there was no question in the eyes of the divorce court who was at fault for the collapse of my marriage. Kayleigh Carson's Instagram account was super helpful since she continued to post shots of my nearly ex-husband kissing her, taking her to dinner, and generally doing a crap ton of #blessed #romantic thing.

I let Sam keep the house, though. I didn't want to be there anymore. I got the 401k and a good deal of cash. That, plus my buyout, put me in a position to say no to alimony. The only tie I wanted with Sam was the tie of our two fantastic kids.

The kids? Well, they were over 18. They could visit who they wanted to at Christmas break.

They shared a dorm at Michigan State. I'd driven up to see them the day after the video because, well, viral video. They were used to their parents being locally famous, but never viral, and never with a hair out of place.

I took them to lunch. I made a grocery trip for them and let them know that I loved them, so did their Dad, but that was going to be happening in separate locations from now on.

"I'm sorry about the viral video thing." Joe and Sam were fraternal twins. Sam Junior had his dad's classic All-American good looks, and Joe had dark hair and looked a little more like me. They were as different as two people who shared the same DNA could be.

"Mom, you're a badass. You've always been a badass." Joe said and hugged me in the parking lot of Armstrong Hall.

"Ha, well, thank you, sweetie."

"Are you going to be okay?" Sam thought he'd need to take care of me in some way, always a bit more worried than Joe, about everything.

"I'm going to be fine. And so is Dad. And so are you. It's just a different fine."

"I'm not calling Kayleigh, mom," Joe said.

I laughed. The woman was like five years older than the boys. Dammit. Sam.

"Dad called, is it okay if..." Sam Junior let it hang there.

"Your relationship with him isn't my business anymore. And, well, I'd say he's a good Dad. Just a not great husband anymore." The boys seemed relieved that I wasn't going to make them pick sides. Which I wasn't.

They could blame who they needed to blame to move on with their lives. They were newborn adults. Gulp.

I had to do the same.

As such, I needed a job and a place to live.

And it had to be a place that allowed pets because I had custody of our pets. To be fair, Sam didn't want either of them.

Bubba Smith was a behemoth canine. He was the biggest, most loving Bull Mastiff. The boys got him from a shelter after he'd been abandoned and hurt. The vet thought he'd probably been run over by a car. I hoped whoever did it was sporting a massive dent in their vehicle and a steamy little nook in hell.

The boys loved him on sight. They named him after Michigan State Spartan football legend Bubba Smith. They walked him, which was more like a slow stroll since Bubba Smith was too big to move fast. Bubba Smith was actually my secret weapon. I knew the boys would visit me wherever I landed, mainly to see their steer-sized dog, if not their dear old mom.

Then, there was Agnes, possibly the snobbiest cat east of the Mississippi.

Agnes just showed up one day and never left. She seemed to know exactly what outfits I should avoid and expressed as much with a sniff whenever I thought I had my look put together. Agnes the Cat was a lot like my mother, judgment-wise, but mercifully, mother was currently judging beachgoer attire on Florida's Gulf Coast.

When Agnes deigned a surface too muddy, cold, or any other non-perfect condition, Bubba Smith was her solution. The big lovable dog would lean his head down, and Agnes would climb on his back to be transported around the house and yard like Cleopatra.

They'd come with me wherever I went, whether Agnes liked it or not.

Finding where to go after I left the house that Sam and I had shared was proving to be a more significant challenge than I'd bargained for.

I spent a depressing few days discovering that television stations weren't hiring anchors who'd gone viral on YouTube for coming unhinged. No matter how many regional Emmys I had, putting me on the air was now a risk to the bottom line. Ah, YouTube... thanks for that.

"So, why'd you leave your last job?" Play the YouTube clip.

I was losing hope that I'd be able to find a job in journalism at all, much less television. And reporting was the only thing I'd ever done.

A call from my Great Aunt Dorothy, who still lived in my tiny hometown, offered a little window of opportunity.

"There's an opening at Your U.P. News. They've got an office right in downtown now." My Aunt Dorothy had always wanted me to come back home, though I hadn't given her an ounce of encouragement since high school.

"It's a bureau, a satellite office, Aunt Dorothy. But thanks. I'll check it out."

"There's so much going on here now! You could cover all the festivities for the All Souls Festival! You would hardly recognize your own hometown. We're about to be booming!"

"Yeah? Well, that's great that the economy is turning around."

Your U.P. News was an online news service for Michigan's Upper Peninsula. They didn't do television. They didn't do an actual print paper. They were all online. They did post videos with some stories. Crappy, shaky, bad audio videos. Of course, I was a shaky unemployed news anchor. I was in the beggars can't be choosers category of employment status and couldn't be too particular.

As steps down went, this was like going from the Detroit Tigers to t-ball.

Though the idea of moving home, for the first time, surprisingly seemed appealing.

Widow's Bay, a place most people in the U.S. didn't even know existed.

My hometown got its name because it was the shipwreck capital of the Great Lakes, which is depressing as heck, I suppose. That also contributed to the idea that it was haunted. That was a tough sell for the economy or tourism.

A town run by widows and haunted by ghosts didn't exactly play well for your Christmas vacation plans or summer break. When other places in Michigan were on Good Morning America as great family getaways, Widow's Bay was great if your idea of a getaway included sad stories of sunken cargo vessels.

Lately, though, that reputation for haunting was being turned into a tourist attraction in an attempt to rev up the local economy. It was like a home improvement project -- if you can't hide it, feature it! I had no idea if the plan was working, but I hoped so for my old friends who owned businesses there.

Widow's Bay was way too small to have a television station; most towns over the Mighty Mac were tiny. And quirky. And packed in snow for 8 months a year.

I'd taken the kids on vacation to Widow's Bay a few times.

And if there was a story worth covering all the way up there. WXYD would usually send me. A few years back, tragedy struck the town, and I was assigned to it.

The station liked to name each tragedy and give the event unique "branding." This one was called the Charity Bus Tragedy.

A group of football dads was on a bus headed for the casino to raise money for the football team. A sudden wind squall combined with an icy bridge swept the bus off the road and into a frigid Lake Superior.

Thirteen dads died. It was terrible, and a lot of my old friends were widowed. Widow's Bay earned its name in this decade thanks to the crash. It even made the national news one night.

And maybe it helped spark the idea of the All Souls Festival that Aunt Dorothy was excited about.

I did the story on the Charity Bus Tragedy, reconnected with my old girlfriends, and the station won an Emmy. A lot of good that Emmy did me now.

I'd tried to leave Widow's Bay behind, mostly. I'd lived my adult life as a troll, or under the bridge, for almost twenty years.

But Aunt Dorothy wasn't a quitter. She was determined to get me back to Widow's Bay. And there was a draw. I did love so many people there. I had friends from growing up that couldn't be rivaled by news colleagues. So, I relented and appeased Aunt Dorothy.

"I'll give them a call about the job, Aunt Dorothy."

I'd dismissed her for decades, but now, for the first time, I was considering her suggestion.

I was desperate. A news job opening in Upper Michigan,

while not ideal, was at least a lead. I had no prospects, and at least I knew the U.P. better than most possible candidates.

There was also another more practical benefit to a job in Widow's Bay: I owned a house there.

I'd bought the family home when my mother retired. I couldn't bear to see it go. We used it in the summer and rented it out when we could. Sam hated it and thought it was a financial mistake. But it was paid off and rent-free for me.

Your U.P. News salaries were likely minuscule. If I took a job there, rent-free would be a big help.

An email and a Skype interview with the main news offices in The Soo, and I was hired within twenty-four hours.

It happened so fast. That must mean it was meant to be.

I'd gone from television anchor in the number one market in Michigan, 14th in the country, to an internet bureau reporter in my tiny hometown at the northern tip of the continental U.S.

I may be headed up geographically speaking, but I was going down, career-wise, like a stone. Even so, my soul felt a little lighter, knowing I was going home. Maybe my lifelong friends were the lifeline I needed as I went from wife and mother to single lady with grown sons.

CHAPTER 2

*W*hen you live in the Upper Peninsula of Michigan, you know what a troll is. Not an internet troll or a troll that tells you how hot you are via Facebook Messenger. No, anyone who lives "under the bridge" is considered a troll if you live above the bridge in the Upper Peninsula.

The bridge is The Mighty Mac, of course.

I sold most of my stuff, stored some stuff, and took only what would fit in the back of my beloved rhino clearcoat colored Jeep Wrangler. Which is gray to the non-Jeep speaking public.

I had a strong desire to pack light in this phase of my life. Plus, I didn't have a ready-made team of heavy lifters at my disposal anymore. If I packed it, I had to haul it.

The Jeep Wrangler was packed pretty tightly, but Grosse Pointe Woods was in my rearview mirror now, and I didn't glance back.

I drove the long stretch up I-75. It was about four hours to the Mackinac Bridge. And then it would be a couple more hours after that until I pulled into Widow's Bay.

Bubba Smith and Agnes were content to take up residence in the back seat as we made our way up north.

It was freeing, thinking that other than my kids, my life was in this Jeep. I'd shed all the junk. Sam was at the top of that rubbish pile.

I listened to the First Wave channel on my satellite radio. I tried to look ahead only. Nostalgia about being a wife and mommy was a trap. I needed to embrace this adventure! Onward!

That said, The Mighty Mac is scary as hell. The five-mile suspension bridge is the only way, other than a ferry or by air, to get to the Upper Peninsula from Michigan's Lower Peninsula.

If you have gephyrophobia, it's the stuff of which nightmares are made.

It was built in the 1950s. Five men died while constructing the behemoth bridge. If you get nervous on the approach, you can call the Mackinac Bridge Authority's Driver's Assistance Program, and a braver soul will drive you across the expanse.

I did not have that particular phobia and found The Mighty Mac to be stunning and beautiful. And the road home.

I clicked over to the AM radio and paid the bridge toll. Channel 530 from the Mackinac Bridge Authority provided facts, history, and weather reports as you traversed the bridge.

For me, it always seemed a gateway to somewhere a little more magical than the rest of the country. It was almost as if the rest of the country didn't know that up here, attached at the top of the contiguous U.S., there was a big, rough, mysterious, and beautiful country all to itself.

For many people, the Upper Peninsula is mysterious. Others have no idea that this is a part of Michigan. The Upper Peninsula contains 29% of the land area of Michigan but just 3% of its total population.

If you wanted wide open spaces, this was the place.

The bridge highway suspended 200 feet over the frigid waters of Lake Michigan. Everyone who's ever seen it knows that if you crash off of it, you're super dead.

I pulled on to the bridge as AM 530 announcers assured me

this would be a calm crossing. On a not so calm day, you gripped the steering wheel until your knuckles ached.

You had two choices, ride the inside lane and listen to the wailing of your tires on the metal grate below, or pick the outside right lane and enjoy the view. I chose the right lane since it was calm. And I glanced out at the blue sky and blue water.

I was always struck by its monstrous size, and honestly, its beauty. It was epic and set against a background of sky, snow, ice, water, or fog, depending on the time of year you crossed.

Maybe the difficulty getting here kept the U.P.'s population small. And the difficulty of thriving here made it tough to stay.

I had stayed away. The pull to come home felt real now, and strong.

As I reached the end of the bridge span, I realized with a strange sense of relief that I was done being a troll.

For now, anyway. The quiet weirdness, the snowy beauty, the otherworldliness of Widow's Bay would be a welcome change. What had driven me away as a teen was now drawing me in.

Maybe it was a mid-life crisis. Whatever it was, I needed old friends now that my perfectly constructed life had fallen apart in chunks.

Widow's Bay was more than an hour away after you crossed The Mighty Mac.

And not long after I reveled in the blue expanse of Lake Michigan as I crossed the bridge on the southern shores of the peninsula, I would be craning my neck to see the first glimpse of the distant waters of Lake Superior.

Widow's Bay was on the shore of Lake Superior and at the base of a mountain. Yep, we had mountains up here too. Just no Vail or Sundance Movie Awards. The Hollywood crowd had never found its way to this patch of sweet powder or fantastic beach.

It wasn't quite evening when I arrived on Main Street of Widow's Bay. Main Street had just about everything: the municipal building, a courthouse, an office building, restaurants, and small mom and pop retail establishments. If you wanted a big box store, you'd need to drive about an hour to The Soo. Widow's Bay, development-wise, was like going back in time.

There was a grand total of three stoplights in Widow's Bay.

After fighting traffic in Detroit, the non-traffic made me smile.

And Aunt Dorothy was right, things looked a little more sparkly right now. Older buildings that had been boarded up were now fixed up.

They really must be going all out for this All Souls Festival. There were also a ton of signs on how to get to Samhain Slopes. There was a brand-new ski resort opening on the ridge.

Hmm. I'd have to check into it. It looked like everything had been rebranded to try to revitalize Widow's Bay. They used to say Widow's Peak, the mountain next to town and the highest point in the county, was too scary a name. Apparently, not now.

The bureau office for Your U.P. News was in the Old School-house Commons building. It used to house all the grades for Widow's Bay students until the 1960s when they built the high school that most county kids, including myself, attended.

The Old School House Commons were now office suites and a workout studio. I'd be reporting there tomorrow, but I took a good look at it as I drove by. It was three stories, all brick, and adorable green awnings hung over the windows. A far cry from WXYD's state-of-the-art studios.

I turned down the familiar street, Birch. And pulled into the driveway of my family's home.

The old Victorian sat on a corner lot. It was beautiful and had been home to several generations of the Nurse family, which was my mom's side.

My Aunt Dorothy was the property manager for me, since my mom flew south, though even Aunt Dorothy had opted to move into a Mature Active neighborhood outside of downtown.

Aunt Dorothy promised that the house was ready for me and waiting.

And so was she.

She was little through the shoulders, short, white-haired, and more intense than just about anyone I'd ever met.

And I had no earthly idea how old she might be.

Aunt Dorothy had been a part of my childhood, the nurturer, when my own mother couldn't be bothered.

It was cold, but she stood in the driveway, waving me in.

"You made it!"

I got out and walked into her hug.

"You're so thin!" She said, and it was true. I'd been on the Divorce Diet, which was a combination of losing your appetite because you were freaking out and freaking out over the idea that a new person would potentially see you naked after decades of being married. It worked like a charm, but I wouldn't recommend it.

The upside was that I was skinnier than I'd been since before having the twins.

"And your hair's completely white!" Aunt Dorothy's hair had been brown with a few gray streaks the last time I'd seen her.

"Got sick of dying. I'm too old to waste time in a beauty salon."

"It looks beautiful."

"Can I help you with your bags? Boxes? Oh, hello." Dorothy was looking at Bubba Smith and Agnes. She nearly always wore pantsuits. She paired the matching pants and blazers with heavy-duty snow boots that came to her calves and could handle whatever weather Widow's Bay was experiencing in that particular second.

"Uh, that's Agnes and Bubba Smith, and no, you can't carry anything." She had to be over eighty but was planning on lifting my stuff into the house. Aunt Dorothy and Agnes exchanged knowing looks. I had no idea what that was about, but if I had to put money on it, I'd say Agnes wasn't happy with Aunt Dorothy's pantsuit. Aunt Dorothy was a politician back in the day, and her wardrobe was Hillary Clinton before Hillary Clinton was the speck of a Rodham. She was a pantsuit wearer before pantsuits were even invented.

"I just need my bag. I'll unpack the rest later. Let's get out of the snow."

A light, fluffy layer had begun to fall, though it was only October. That was the U.P for you.

"We haven't had renters since August. I had it cleaned after they left, and then last week, when you said you were coming home, the service came and freshened it. It should be all set!"

"Thank you, Aunt Dorothy, I'm sure it's fine."

We walked in the front door. Bubba Smith carried Agnes in and disappeared into the big house. A flood of memories overwhelmed me for a moment. Good and bad.

"The electrical, plumbing, and Wi-Fi should all be tip-top."

"Score one for you knowing about Wi-Fi!" I said to my great aunt.

"Oh, yes, for sure. I mean, who wants to use all their data to play Trivia Crack?" Aunt Dorothy said it without a hint of irony. She may be ancient, but her mind was sharp as a tack. The woman was with it.

"You know where everything is, of course."

"Sure, and thank you. Having you take care of the rentals for the seasons has been, well, probably too much to ask."

"Nonsense. I'd do some updating though, there's wallpaper in the dining room that I think you can date to the Truman administration."

"We'll see. I'm not sure how long I'm going to be here."

"Oh, pshaw. You're going to love being here with your old friends."

"The job prospects for me right now are slim to none, so you might be right on me staying, friends or not."

"I've got to run honey, I've got a DLC meeting. If we don't finish our meeting in time for everyone to get home for Jeopardy, it gets ugly."

"You're still doing that club?" From what I understood, The Widow's Bay Distinguished Ladies Club or the DLC was nearly as old as the town. The club raised money for everything anyone needed, and I was pretty sure they also gossiped about anything everyone did.

"Oh, yes, I am. We're getting smaller, dying left and right, you know. It's time you stepped up on that."

"Aunt Dorothy, as a journalist, I can't be affiliated with groups that have agendas. I have to be unbiased."

"Oh please, like bringing potato salad is an agenda! We'll talk about it later. Like I said if we miss that silver fox, Alex Trebek, Maxine gets cranky!" She smiled at me and waved me off. The last thing I needed was to spend time at meetings planning bake sales and assigning covered dish duties for the Arbor Day Picnic, journalist or not.

"Do you need a ride anywhere?"

"No, parked my 300 on the street, there, see?"

"Yes, be careful walking, it's getting slick."

"This is nothing, you've been down south too long."

I watched as she made it to her car.

I looked around the house. The old Victorian home was stuck in time. I could see myself updating kitchen cabinets, removing wallpaper, and maybe making it mine instead of my parents' old house or a summer renter.

It was an HGTV fixer-upper dream come true, really. Good bones would be the phrase to use, I suppose.

I made quick work of unloading my Jeep. I decided to take the master bedroom instead of my old room. There were three others. I felt a little strange that it was just me in this place. But I was determined to make this work.

I did wonder where the Pinterest boards were for this. If you were just engaged, just married, or a new mommy of little ones, there were a million different cute ideas. Not so much for me at this stage of life.

Maybe I should start an empty nester divorcee board. It could have "He got the girlfriend, and I got the 401K" written in scrolly letters on a blackboard. Great recipe ideas for one!

Ugh. I needed to stay off Pinterest.

I looked around for Bubba Smith and Agnes. They'd arranged themselves nicely in the dining room. Bubba must have dragged their mutual fluff pile that I'd carted from downstate into the corner of our new digs. Bubba did everything for Agnes. That cat was haughty as hell, and the dog was her minion.

We thought the dining room was a good spot since you're probably going to be eating alone in the kitchen most days.

"Don't be so sure. Maybe I'll turn into a swinging single."

Not with that giant hair on your chinny chin chin.

"WHAT?" I reached up and felt it. Ew. Ugh. Where had that one come from?

Told you.

I was about to grab the tweezers from my bag when I stopped and turned back to Agnes. Had that cat talked to me? Had I answered back?

Yes, now leave me alone. I need my beauty rest, so do you by the looks of those bags.

"No need to be so rude." I could give as good as I got.

I shook my head and turned off the light in the dining room. I was now communicating, in English, with my snarky cat.

This was how bat crap crazy started. I was sure that this was all in my head, and Agnes was sure it wasn't. I didn't have too much time to freak out about it because luckily, my cell phone buzzed.

"Are you settled in?"

It was Tatum.

Though I'd left Widow's Bay, I had stayed close with a few

friends. Tatum was one of those BFFs who, even though I didn't see every day, when we were together, it was as if no time had passed.

There were several of us that bonded here in Widow's Bay, and no matter where life took us, that bond stuck.

Tatum McGowan ran the Frog Toe Micro Brewery in Widow's Bay. Her husband had died in the Charity Bus Tragedy. Their son was off to college these days. And Tatum wasn't my only friend who'd lost a husband on that trip. It bonded the women here in a way that only shared trauma can.

I'd been here to cover the story and hold my friends' hands as they became widows.

It was the worst tragedy the town had seen since the sinking of the SS Bannockburn, but that was way before my time. That was an old ghost story. The bus crash was fresh trauma.

The last few years had been tough on Widow's Bay, but Tatum was tougher. All the women here were.

It was funny, most of my old friends were in the same place as I was right now. On our own. Maybe being here, in town, was exactly where I needed to be as I navigated brand new singlehood.

"You all moved in?" Tatum asked. I could hear the crowd in the background. Frog Toe was happening tonight.

"Yes, though, this place needs a makeover. Sounds like you're busy."

"Yeah, Monday night is the new Friday night here, and this place is jam-packed with Hoopsters. I can't even imagine what All Souls Festival's going to look like. I may need you to sling drinks, sister."

Tatum had coined the phrase, Hoopster. Hipsters that live in the U.P. were Hoopsters to her. Hoopsters were discovering the Frog Toe and its magical craft beers, and now more people were starting to notice. Good for Tatum!

"How's tomorrow night looking?"

"Busy, but who cares? I'll call the girls, and we'll sit around the cauldron to celebrate your freedom and return to The Bay."

Tatum's Frog Toe had an iron cauldron that featured prominently in the décor. Guests enjoyed sitting around the fire and speculating about the special powers of Tatum's microbrews.

"What's your take on this All Souls Festival, is it going to work?"

"I can't say for sure, but Candy and The Chamber of Commerce say it's going to be huge, like bigger than Christmas in Frankenmuth."

"Wow, I'll have to get up to speed! See you tomorrow night."

"Great. Good luck on your first day at UP Your News."

"Hello, it's Your U.P. News."

"Whatever."

Tatum was tough as nails, and she helped make me tougher. It was also good to know that ultimately, if I had a squad, it was here, in Widow's Bay. No matter how far I had roamed.

CHAPTER 3

For my entire professional life hair, makeup, outfits, and jewelry were part of my uniform. I blow-dried my naturally wavy hair into submission, I dyed away any random gray, I exfoliated, I buffed, I polished, I waxed, I contoured and did every damn thing a person could do to their face to have it look TV-ready.

The clothes? Every single skirt suit set available on planet Earth in every color hung in my closet. And there were accessories to match.

I wasn't a label person. I didn't care if it was a designer brand. In the anchorwoman game, you needed volume. I'd donated my power suits to a charity in Detroit that coached formerly homeless women entering the job market. I hoped that the power suits would get a second life helping people. I, however, didn't miss one thread of my television wardrobe.

Even before the Sam meltdown, my statement necklaces felt like they were choking me. The care and feeding of a television newswoman were becoming harder to manage every passing day. I'd grown out of my life. Maybe Sam had pushed me in a direction I might have gone anyway, out of television.

That didn't mean he wasn't a complete douchenozzle.

I woke up early. I wasn't used to the house or its sounds, and I was excited to start something new. I showered and realized my entire "get ready" process had gone from over an hour-and-a-half to under thirty minutes. Saving over an hour a day? Hell, maybe I'd learn a foreign language in my spare time.

It was incredibly liberating to get ready for my first day of work at Your U.P. News. Sure, I might file a Facebook Live report here or there, but mostly, I was writing stories for the internet. Massive hairspray usage wasn't a job requirement anymore.

It was cold in Widow's Bay unless it was July, and I had prepared. I pulled on jeans, a black turtleneck, a cardigan, and Uggs. I had a brand-new full-length parka stashed in the car. I suspected it would be my new best friend in the coming months. I also loaded the Jeep with more layers I could pile on as needed, including a Stormy Kromer fur-lined hat with ear flaps. I may be new to Your U.P. News, but I wasn't new to UP weather. It could be a bitch, but so could I.

I made sure Bubba Smith and Agnes had food and water. But I didn't make my escape to work before Agnes weighed in on my new, simpler, and more casual personal style.

Lipstick and mascara, that's it?

"Yeah, got a problem with that?" I'd decided my brain was coping with change by hashing out my life with the cat. That was fine, right? Not cause for concern or mental health professionals?

Letting yourself go at forty. Tragic.

"I'm not forty yet. And I'm not letting myself go."

I decided this conversation was over. It really felt like Agnes was talking to me, but come on, even I knew that it had to be me projecting. I was managing massive life changes with a feline sounding board. Yeah. That had to be it. Either way, talking to my cat was one thing, but being late to work because she didn't like my style, well... that was crossing the line.

"Bubba, you deal with her. I'm headed to work." Agnes turned her nose up at me. I left the haughty cat to her vassal. I knew that the two of them would be just fine without me.

The drive to my new office was less than five minutes long, even with the fresh snowfall. While other places in the country called off school for snow days, in the Upper Peninsula, the kids got on snowmobiles and got to class. A few inches in October wasn't even a blip on the radar.

Pauline Rogers owned the Old School House Commons building. She was a real estate agent, a fitness instructor, and another old friend from high school.

At this early hour, she was teaching a fitness class before she'd head upstairs to her office to sell sell sell and buy buy buy. Her perfectly fit frame was a testament to the fact that this former cheerleader never sat still. Any calorie that made its way to her was burned up like tissue paper on a lit match.

Pauline's indoor cycling class was just finishing. I'd arranged to get the keys to my new office from her. She saw me and finished the cool-down stretches.

"Open those hips! Release those shoulders. Great job, every-one, see you at seven!"

She ran over to me with her trademark high energy, as if she hadn't just led an intense workout.

"You MADE it!" Pauline was another friend who'd been widowed in the last few years, but her husband had died of a heart attack, not the bus crash.

"I did."

"I'd hug you, but I'm so sweaty."

"How long have you been doing the cycling classes?"

"I had to switch it up. Last month I tried to get them to do this CrossFit style workout. There was a full-scale rebellion."

"I can't blame them! CrossFit? No way. Maybe cycling, though -- do you have space for one more?"

"For sure! Come tomorrow. It'd be a good way for you to

meet people. Most of the women in town are in or out of here at some point in the week."

"Maybe, I will." I had always exercised; it was how I lost the weight after the twins. But the last few months had been about survival, not working out. This was a new life and a new chance to do things just for me. Take that empty nest!

I liked the idea of doing the things I wanted to do, not what the kids needed, or the television station required, or my husband wanted.

"Your office is on the second floor, end of the hall. Wi-Fi is hooked up and paid for by your newsroom, so if you need anything else, text me!" I nodded thanks, and she headed back to her sweaty students.

I walked the flight up to the office and saw the Your U.P. News logo on the door. It would be an effort not to think of it as Up Your News, thank you very much, Tatum.

The office for the Bureau consisted of three small rooms. I walked into the largest, which had a desk and computer. It also had a large window from which I could see down Main Street.

Banners were being hung for the upcoming All Souls Festival. There was no such festival here when I was growing up. I wondered again if this inaugural attempt to inspire tourism in Widow's Bay would work. We'd see soon enough.

I looked around my new space. There was a conference table in the other smaller room, and then there was a smaller area that could maybe serve as an editing bay area if I was going to shoot and edit video.

I hoped I'd be able to show Your U.P. News that they were getting a bargain in me. I had always reported, written, and even sometimes edited my own stuff. I'd have to do it all now, though, because the staff of Your U.P. News Widow's Bay Bureau consisted of me… and me.

I determined the place needed a coffee maker, a mini-fridge, and a small microwave if it was going to be my home away from home. I had no reason to rush out of the office anymore, and if I was knee-deep in work, I didn't have to feel guilty. That was new and would take some getting used to.

I sat down at the desk, picked up the office phone and called into the newsroom, located an hour away in Sault Ste. Marie.

"Newsroom."

"Hi, this is Marzie Nowak, I'm calling in for my first day."

"Oh yeah, you're the new Paul."

"Excuse me?"

"Paul, he was our bureau guy before, fired."

A quick vision, like a fast forward, appeared in front of me. There was a man at this same desk, playing internet poker. Paul, I knew it, and couldn't tell you why. I supposed that's why he didn't work out.

I blinked hard and focused on the call.

"Oh, they told me to check in with Justin Lemorre." I had Skype interviewed with the owner of Your U.P. News, Garrett DeWitt. I knew he was handsome, and I suspected he had some money. Dewitt was financing this whole online news thing as some sort of pet project, I guessed. He said, getting a seasoned journalist like me was a coup. But then again, that's what you said when you didn't pay much. I hadn't met anyone in real life at this new job of mine.

"Yep, he's the main assignment editor. I'll transfer you."

I waited a second. Most producers in small towns were young, right out of college, and to be honest, clueless about what it meant to go out of the newsroom and turn a story.

But I was trying not to prejudge Justin Lemorre. He'd be my main lifeline to the newsroom.

"Welcome to the team, we've got a murder."

"Justin?"

"Yep. Scanner traffic out your way, on uh, Birch. You know where that is?" Considering I lived on Birch, that would be a yes.

"Yes, right off the main drag here in town."

"Good."

"What are they saying on the scanner?" Dead bodies happened all the time; most of the time, that didn't mean murder. I was floored to think that my quiet little small-town street was a murder scene. I'd just left the big city for goodness sake. Maybe Justin was overreacting to scanner traffic. That was way more likely.

"They're calling for a crew with a camera." That meant authorities were collecting evidence. If a person died of a suspected heart attack or cancer, no one called for cameras and evidence collection. Something at the scene must mean the police suspected foul play. Maybe Justin did know a thing or two about listening to a police scanner.

"On it."

"And get me something fast. Beating everyone else online is our main thing, I'm sure Garrett told you that. There should be a logo thing for your dashboard, it will get you through most police lines."

I looked. Sure, enough there, it was on the desk.

"Got it."

"Email me your story, pics, everything. You'll learn how to directly upload to YourUPNews.com later, but right now, we need you out there fast. Keep me in the loop, Mary."

He hung up before I could tell him it was Marzie.

Okay then, it was off to Birch street for a murder. I could scarcely believe it. There were murders every day in Detroit, but Widow's Bay? Usually, hunting accidents or high cholesterol were at the door when death came knocking around here.

I drove my Jeep as fast as I could to Birch. I had the logo-ed sign displayed on my dashboard. It was a printed sheet of copy paper, run through a laminator. Hopefully, it was just official enough in this neck of the woods to get me access.

The address was only two blocks from my own house.

I parked, made sure I had my phone and a notepad and walked toward the house.

I also thought I knew who lived here or used to anyway, the town grouch, Lottie Bradbury.

Lottie was debatably the oldest but verifiably the crankiest person in Widow's Bay.

But I still had a hard time believing that I was headed to a murder scene. Lottie Bradbury had probably fallen down the basement stairs or something.

I wondered if writing the obituary would also be on my plate. Any news that happened here was now in my wheelhouse.

A police vehicle and a rescue squad truck from the fire department were parked in the driveway.

Crime scene tape blocked the front walk. I tried not to roll my eyes. Odds were that the crime tape was entirely unnecessary, and someone was just itching to play with crime scene tape.

Who could possibly want to murder an ancient, cranky lady?

Neighbors milled around, holding their coffee cups, and craning their necks to see what was happening at Lottie Bradbury's.

I recognized some of the faces. Not a lot had changed in Widow's Bay in twenty years. Steam from the coffee and breath wafted up into the cold air. As the saying went, there were two seasons in Michigan's Upper Peninsula, winter, and orange barrel season.

"Hey, Marzie, you back in town?" It was Chet Gerwick. He'd been a resident of Widow's Bay his whole life.

"Working for Your U.P. News these days."

"Yeah, I wondered what was going to happen to you after I saw you on YouTube, hilarious. Uh, I mean, I'm sorry."

"Yeah, not my best moment."

"Their loss is our gain! Do you know what happened?" Chet pointed to the crime scene tape.

"No, just got here. I'm sure it was natural causes, though, right? I mean, she wasn't a crime lord or drug dealer, right?"

"No, but she was mean enough to be one if you ask me. Lottie had to be at least eighty, right? But old age did not mellow her." Chet asked me about Lottie's age, and I shrugged. I didn't know. I just knew Lottie was known for her unpleasant disposition. Her face was always pinched into a scowl.

"Well, let me know when they open the shed. She's got at least three of my kid's soccer balls in there."

"She's still doing that?"

Lottie confiscated so many balls that innocently bounced into her yard. It probably looked like a PE locker in that shed.

"She probably still has my hula hoop from 1990."

"Yeah, it was like her job to ruin the backyard fun."

"Everyone needs a hobby, I guess. 'If that ball bounces into my yard, I'm keeping it.' Probably should be on her headstone," I said, and Chet laughed. It was strange in a way to be reporting in such a small town. In the big city, the subjects of my stories were never people I knew, much less neighbors.

An officer walked out of the house, and I knew right away who it was.

Officer Byron DeLoof. He had been two grades older than me in high school. He was a nice guy, if not a little clumsy and awkward back in the day.

He actually looked whiter than I remembered. Maybe it was the assignment? He walked as fast as his belly, and the little snow cover would allow. His face was more serious than I'd ever seen it.

"If it isn't the famous anchor Marzenna Nowak!" DeLoof cracked a little smile and quickly extinguished it. He was working hard to be official.

"Yep, good to see you, Loof. Working here now." I flashed my Your U.P. News i.d. badge.

"Cool."

"That's a lot of crime scene tape you have out there on the walk."

"It is a crime scene." They'd taped the entire yard off, front, and back. The yellow ribbons were a stark contrast to the fresh snow. I noticed footprints in the front yard in the otherwise immaculate snow. Were those steps clues? Or had the small-town cops walked all over the place already?

"Loof, Lottie Bradbury was eighty if she was a day. What was it a stroke? A fall?"

"No, the initial surveying of the crime scene indicates something else," he put an emphasis on crime.

"Well?"

"Lottie may have fallen, but she landed neck first onto a knife or something incredibly jagged." I winced at that description.

"You're telling me she was murdered?" Justin's ability to assess police scanner traffic went up another notch.

"Yes, that's what I'm telling you."

"Who found the body?" I was writing answers down and getting my phone in position.

"It was a UPS guy. He said that Lottie was addicted to QVC. The brown truck was here just about every morning. When she didn't answer the door to sign for the package, he was concerned. Looked in the window and boom."

I opened my phone's camera app and hit video to record.

"Say it again? The UPS guy found her." The UPS delivery man must have left the tracks in the snow. DeLoof noticed I was recording and straightened up a little. He cleared his throat.

"The dispatcher received a call to this address that delivery personnel observed that the female who allegedly lived at this domicile was on the kitchen floor and appeared to be stationary."

"The UPS guy found Lottie dead on the kitchen floor. Can you talk normally?"

"In my official capacity, I cannot." I sighed. For some reason, authorities started speaking a different language when it was time to talk to the press.

"Fine, what time was that?"

"Zero-eight-hundred hours." I tried not to roll my eyes.

"Okay, so eight a.m. How old was Lottie Bradbury?"

"I'm not allowed to confirm the victim's name."

"You just told me it was her two seconds ago."

DeLoof grimaced at his mistake.

"Darn it. We just don't get this stuff very often. I'm rusty."

"Look, how long was she dead, do you think?"

"At least a few hours. Probably happened overnight based on our initial investigation."

"Hmm."

"And don't report her name until I say you can, okay? Or I'll be up a creek with Chief Bud."

Bud Marvin was the Chief of Police and Byron DeLoof's boss.

"I won't until you say it is okay. But you know everyone in town already knows. Look, even a couple of DLC are here." I pointed to three white-haired women bundled together and gawking alongside the neighbors, including my Aunt Dorothy.

"You know locals have taken to calling them The Crones," DeLoof whispered under his breath.

"I didn't. Thanks for the tip."

If the Distinguished Ladies, or Crones, were here, then the news would soon be everywhere. Who needed the internet when you had the DLC?

"We're working on next of kin. You wouldn't happen to know if she has a family?"

"No idea." At some point, Lottie herself was a member of the DLC, I thought. But maybe I was wrong. It had been a while since I was up on all the local daily comings and goings.

"Do you know if she has enemies?" Loof asked me with a hopeful look in his eye. The seasoned investigator was fishing for clues from me? This didn't bode well.

"You're kidding, right? You know she's been mean to just about everyone in this town. But stab-her-in-the-neck enemies? That seems like an overreaction. I mean, she's famous for keeping soccer balls, but murder?"

"That's what I thought too. Bud is on the way over. You better get back away from my crime scene, or he'll have my head."

"Fine."

"Marzie, do you think WXYD will come out?"

"News-wise, I'm probably it, Loof. Sorry to disappoint you. It's too far a drive. They barely made it here when the bus crashed." That was the most significant news the town had seen in decades. But weather, terrain, and distance made sending a reporter to Widow's Bay logistically tricky unless it was something that could go national like the bus crash.

"Darn, I like that one reporter, Kayleigh Carson." Of course, he did, everyone liked her.

"Loof, you have any clues you want to share with me? Like how'd they get in? And is there a danger to the public? Do we have a homicidal maniac loose in Widow's Bay?"

"Come on now, no. We're all safe. There's no maniac. I don't think." Loof didn't look too sure, but he never did look too sure.

"I can see the headline now. WBPD don't *think* there's a maniac on the loose." I upward inflected the word think to make my point.

Loof pulled up his pants by the belt and pursed his lips at me.

"We'll get it solved. You put that in your story. Also, anyone with any information can call me." Confidence that they'd solve it, combined with a blanket plea for random clues… not a great combo, but I didn't want to bust Loof's chops too much on this first day.

"Will do. How much longer you going to be?"

"Bud's got to clear the scene after they take the body to county for the autopsy."

As if on cue, two workers from the coroner's office wheeled

out the body of Lottie Bradbury, wrapped in a bright yellow tarp. Out of respect for the dead, I only took a few photos of the exterior of the house, the crime tape, and the footprints in the snow. None of poor Lottie.

The sheriff showed up as the departed Lottie departed.

"Chief Marvin! Can you confirm that Lottie Bradbury was murdered in her kitchen?" I pointed my phone camera toward Bud Marvin, but he brushed past me and into the house. It was worth a try anyway. Where Loof was chatty Bud Marvin was a John Wayne type. I didn't have any history with Bud; he was a transplant to Widow's Bay. I'd have to rely on Loof for the scoop on this investigation. Luckily Loof liked to talk.

That was what I'd learned as a reporter. People liked to talk even when they knew they shouldn't. I could always find someone to give me a nugget on whatever story I was working. I knew FBI agents who were as chatty as the neighborhood gossips.

"We're just about done processing, Marzie," Loof said and tried to move me along and away from the sidewalk.

I looked around and noticed that the gawkers were getting cold, so they were starting to disperse. The initial curiosity was satisfied. Lottie Bradbury was dead. She'd confiscated her last kickball and badminton shuttlecock.

I wondered how skilled Loof and crew were at collecting evidence. Widow's Bay didn't usually have a need for CSI Miami style skills.

At the beginning of my career, I was a general assignment reporter. Meaning I did a story on whatever happened that day. In Detroit, back then, I'd covered a murder a day for WXYD. It taught me a lot, including knowing that the best time to get interviews was right now.

Bystanders and gawkers wanted to know what the police knew, so they'd trade information with me to get their own personal scoop.

I'd need a neighbor or a friend of Lottie, someone who was saddened, shocked, or even afraid. Otherwise, I just had Loof's official statement, and that was a weak story.

Aunt Dorothy and her friends caught my eye.

They were looking intently at the house and watching the coroner van as it rolled away with Lottie in the back.

The DLC membership included the town's oldest widows. They always brought a covered dish and an uncovered opinion to any event in Widow's Bay. I marched toward them and hoped Aunt Dorothy and company would tell me more about Lottie. Surely that had two or three cents about a murder on Birch Street.

Widow's Bay had a lot of widows right now. Old widows, middle-aged widows, and now sadly, young widows. Women in Widow's Bay were winding up alone, just like the old Crones of the Distinguished Ladies Club. It was a thought that chilled me a little, but I shook it off. I had a story to get done. I wanted Justin to realize that I was a good reporter. I didn't need hair, makeup, and a photographer to get the job done. I also didn't need supervision. The older I got, the more I resented being micromanaged. I'd report the heck out of my first assignment, and if anyone had a quote or insight into Lottie Bradbury, it would be one of these ladies.

Aunt Dorothy was the most "with it" of the DLC. She was a take-charge woman and always had been. She stood with her arms linked on both sides with Mrs. Elsie Faulkner and Mrs. Maxine Proctor.

"It's terrible," said Maxine Proctor.

"Yeah, it is. Lottie was a friend of yours, right, Aunt Dorothy?"

"We used to be closer, not lately, though," Dorothy said.

"Really, I thought I saw her at one of your Life After Death Club support group things. The one I covered after the bus crash?" The Life After Death Club was the old women's grief support group. The women in front of me organized a fundraiser or spearheaded a group for just about every eventuality of life in Widow's Bay. Well, they used to, before Facebook made groups virtual instead of something that met in a church basement.

"We kind of grew apart from Lottie, the last few years."

I wished I knew more of Lottie's story. And it was a shame, now that the woman wasn't here to tell it.

"How old was she? Late seventies? Eighty?" I suspected she was around the age of my Aunt. Though I could only speculate on her age as well. She'd always been an older lady in my mind. I never knew her young. In fact, I don't think anyone in town remembered the DLC when they were young. Or even not widowed.

Dorothy looked me in the eyes.

"Try ninety-seven," Dorothy said.

"She was one of the young ones," Elsie said. She looked the saddest of the three as she craned her neck to see the house behind me.

I swallowed hard. The young ones? Just how the hell old were The Crones?

"I had no idea. We were all thinking maybe she was eighty. Ninety-seven, wow. Can I ask you a few questions about her life? It would really help me write my story for You U.P. News."

"You know now you're going to have to step up," While Elsie was focused on the body being driven away, Maxine Proctor directed this strange comment to me. Her eyes were like little laser beams boring into my skull.

"What?" Maybe Maxine had some sort of dementia, heck maybe Elsie did too. I started to lose hope that these women were a good source of a quote for my story. Aunt Dorothy stepped in and made at least a little sense.

"Well, nothing is holding them back now, thank the goddess! That's one good thing." Elsie was talking, but it wasn't to me.

"Holding who back? I'm not following either of you."

"Oh, you know, civic duty, it's time for your generation to

take over. You and your friends. We've got the Life After Death Club, the Main Street Beautification Committee, Founders Weekend. There's a lot of opportunities to get involved, especially with the new All Souls festivities. Like I told you. You could be more like Candy." Candy was a friend, a super volunteer-y friend. I wasn't volunteer-y. Aunt Dorothy rattled off a few of the million groups the ladies participated in and said it with a smile on her face.

Did they want me to join the Distinguished Ladies and take up knitting or bake sales? Aunt Dorothy and her two friends were nodding in agreement as she went on and on.

"Ladies, I don't have a clue what you're talking about. I'm trying to learn a little more about Lottie."

"Hmm, she loved her tea, right, Dorothy?" Elsie deferred to Aunt Dorothy, and she nodded to her friend.

"You're soft-pedaling this generation. I say rip it off! Like a bandage!" Maxine directed the comment to Aunt Dorothy, and none of what they were saying made a lick of sense. These three had always been a bit wacky, and in the years I'd been gone, the wacky factor had grown exponentially.

"We've got arrangements to make." Aunt Dorothy said by way of explanation for her ending the conversation.

"I need to find her cat," Maxine said to the other ladies. Her expression had shifted from bossy in my direction to worry over Lottie's house pets.

"Shh... that cat's probably long gone, it was older than we are." Aunt Dorothy nodded to me, and as a group, they linked arms. "Good luck with your story, dear."

She and her friends turned away from me and the scene of the crime.

The Crones were losing it. That was all there was to it. I watched as the ladies disappeared around the corner, still walking with arms linked.

I really didn't have time to decipher the weird comments.

My chance at any good interviews with friends or neighbors was slipping away as people got colder.

I needed to finish up and get back to the office. Justin said first online was the goal. I wished I had more, but for now, a murder in Widow's Bay was going to have to be a story with just the basic facts.

The Crones, as Loof said they were now called, were just batty. It apparently came with being a thousand years old.

My phone buzzed. It was Justin in the newsroom. I picked it up.

"So what? Push alert? Natural causes? Give me an update."

I recited the basic facts.

"I'll have the story filed in an hour."

"Thirty minutes." It used to be working in the news, even television news, you had at least a little time. The news was on at six, or the paper came out in the morning, but since all news was online, all deadlines were immediate no matter where you worked.

There were push alerts for the app, and updates for Facebook

You had a hot second from getting the information to getting it out to the readers.

I thought the pressure might be a little looser here up north since I was the only game going. In Detroit, there were at least three or four outlets at just about every news event.

"I'm the only one here. You'll have the scoop even it takes me forty minutes."

"Just hurry up and send me a few pictures," Justin said. He was not a warm fuzzy person, I decided.

"On it." I took a few more pictures of the house. It was my first day, and I did want to be sure that Your U.P. News had all they needed.

I snapped a wide shot, and then I zoomed in on the footprints in Lottie's yard. It was a fine line between covering the story and being gruesome, and I didn't know where Your U.P. News drew that line.

I had what I needed on this, and it was time to get going.

I turned to walk back to the Jeep and felt something squish under my feet. I looked down to see a small rag doll, laying half on the sidewalk and half in Lottie's lawn. It was dusted with snow and outside the copious crime tape. There was a piece of cloth safety pinned to the chest, and a tuft of fuzz on its faceless head.

It struck me as odd, considering Lottie confiscated all implements of play that crossed her threshold. This toy somehow left on the lawn, mocked the old woman's disdain for fun.

The doll was out of place in more ways than one. It looked old-fashioned. I picked it up. The thing escaped Lottie's net. Some little girl probably thought it was a lost cause, though. I tossed the doll in the back of the Jeep. Maybe I'd pair it with the owner if I came out here for follow up stories.

I took one last look at Lottie's house. It was getting quiet. Whatever Budd Marvin and his team needed from Lottie's house, they'd gotten apparently.

I needed to get the first story on the record about the Murder of Lottie Bradbury. No witnesses, no suspects, and at this point no motive. But according to Loof, the public was totally safe.

I got back to my new office in downtown Widow's Bay. I docked my laptop and got to work.

I started typing, and my phone vibrated. It was Loof.

"We found a nephew. He's aware now that Lottie is deceased. You're good to report that it was Lottie."

"Dead Loof, the word is dead. Hey, I heard from The Crones she was 97." I knew Loof thought Lottie was a lot younger like I had.

"Didn't look it."

"Agree, thanks for the go-ahead," I said.

"You're welcome, oh, and welcome home, murder on the first day," Loof said.

"Yeah, never would have predicted that," I said, and we ended the call. I quickly wrote up my story.

SUBJECT: *Elderly Widow's Bay woman, found murdered in her home.*

Widow's Bay, MI - The body of an elderly woman was found in her Birch Street home Monday. Wounds in her neck indicated that she may have been stabbed.

Widow's Bay Police say a UPS driver arrived at the home with a package and found Lottie Bradbury's body in the kitchen. Friends say Bradbury was 97-years old.

"We're not sure who would have a reason to do this." Police Officer Byron DeLoof said in an interview at the scene.

Authorities talked to neighbors who live on the quiet Birch Street community. None saw or heard anything out of the ordinary. Authorities estimate the murder occurred sometime after midnight but hope to pinpoint the time after an official autopsy is completed.

Investigators won't elaborate on a possible motive and aren't disclosing if they have any witnesses or suspects.

They say nothing appeared to be stolen from Bradbury's home.

Neighbors described Lottie Bradbury as a fixture on the block.

"She lived there before we moved in," said Chet Gerwick, a longtime neighbor of Lottie Bradbury.

"It's scary to think we've got a murderer loose in Widow's Bay. I'm going to be keeping my kids indoors," said Shelly Prater, another Birch Street neighbor.

Though authorities won't speculate on possible suspects, in this case, they did assure the public that there's no larger safety threat.

"There's no reason to believe that anyone else is in danger," said DeLoof.

They won't comment on whether there were signs of forced entry at the Bradbury home.

The coroner will complete an official autopsy in the coming days.

If you have any information on this crime, you're asked to call CrimeBlocker or the Widow's Bay Police Department. Tipsters can remain anonymous.

I HAD several unusable quotes about Lottie's nasty disposition, and her propensity to destroy backyard fun, but she'd just been murdered. Even though "Old Lady That Everyone Hated Found Dead" was probably an accurate headline, I couldn't very well use that.

I looked at the copy I'd written. It was short and raised a million questions.

I wanted to know more about Lottie. I wondered if the relative DeLoof had found would be able to write an obituary.

Lottie Bradbury's death was a mystery for sure, but her life was proving to be just as mysterious. How had she lived so long? Why had she fallen out with the other Distinguished Ladies?

I filed the story and knew I could come up with at least one or two follow-ups if I did a little digging.

I would find out more about Lottie, and maybe that would help me figure out if this was random violence or if there was something more to the murder of the old woman.

I knew the answers about Lottie's life were with The Crones.

I didn't believe for a minute they were older than Lottie, but I did think they could help fill in the blanks. There had to be more to Lottie's life than shaking her gnarled finger at cavorting children.

CHAPTER 4

J filed the murder story before noon and checked in with Justin.

"I'll follow up on the investigation as needed, and thought I'd work on an obit for the victim if nothing comes in from family. She was once fairly prominent here."

"Fine, but that's going to have to wait. I emailed you all the events and news releases for things you might want to cover today in Chippewa County. Let me know what ones you think look the best for coverage."

"Any opinions on that?" I knew what television news stations wanted but didn't presume that I knew what You U.P. News was after for the website each day.

"Jobs, traffic, crime of course, and cats. If you can put a cat in every story, our web traffic would be through the roof."

"I'll see what I can do." I thought about the wisdom of turning Agnes into a kitty model. Then I realized she'd probably never stoop to that. She'd need an agent and a gig in New York or Milan to make it worth her while.

Justin then said something I considered music to my ears.

"Mary, we trust our reporters. That comes from Garret

DeWitt on down. You're in the community. You're going to know better than I am." I had to admit that it was refreshing, ridiculously refreshing.

"Thanks, Justin, looking at this list, and based on jobs being important to your readers this event with the councilwoman and the ski resort opening, I think I'll head over to that and write something up. And the name's Marzie."

"Oh, sorry, Marzie, that's a new one. Check in with me later."

I was pleasantly surprised. In twenty-years of television, I had been micromanaged and consulted to death. Typical reporters have a couple hours if they're lucky, to get to a story, conduct interviews, and shoot video. And rarely did you have the freedom to decide what you'd cover on any given day. In Detroit, if a story idea wasn't focus-grouped, labeled breaking news or weather, I had to beg to cover it.

Maybe what I'd lost in salary I'd gained in autonomy. At my experience level, a career with fewer meetings, hands-off management, and more trust was like gold. Except for the actual gold part.

Who knows, maybe Your U.P. News could be a career highlight instead of a step-down?

I looked at the news release sent from the Office of Council Woman Candy Hitchcock.

Candy was a year older than me in school. She was the president of the student council, the head cheerleader, and was about as competitive as they came. We weren't exactly BFFs, but I had to say, the more I knew her, the more I respected her drive and her total commitment to making our hometown great. Even though I wondered if it was doomed to fail. The All Souls Festival was trying to capitalize instead of downplaying our creepy history. I didn't know if that was possible.

Even so, she'd give it her all.

I looked at Candy's campaign website, CandyHitchcock.com.

Her resume revealed that since high school, she'd continued

serving as the president of everything from Moms to Moms, to PTA, to football boosters, and she'd been elected to the Widow's Bay town council five years ago.

I'd interviewed her after her husband died in the Charity Bus Tragedy. She was poised, beautiful, and despite having gone through a terrible loss, there wasn't a hair out of place. She also bore a particular burden: just like many of the new initiatives in town, I'd heard the ill-fated bus trip was her idea. That had to be tough to live with.

Candy Hitchcock was currently running for Mayor of Widow's Bay, and today could be a big step in getting votes.

According to the news release, Candy was going to be cutting the ribbon at Samhain Slopes Resort along with the owners, investors, and other area bigwigs.

Samhain Slopes Resort had been built over the last few years. Growing up it we called it Widow's Peak, where locals skied in the winter, including me. There was a rope tow to get up top and bonfire at the bottom, but that was about the extent of the development.

That all changed in the last two years. Significant money and development were underway to turn Samhain Slopes Resort into a winter wonderland ski destination.

I hadn't seen it. But I'd heard from friends that the lodge was massive. They'd also done a ton of infrastructure upgrades, so non-four-wheel drive vehicles could make it up the always snowy roads.

Samhain Slopes Resort was situated on the side of the highest peak in the county. As I rounded the curve of the mountain, I realized that GPS wouldn't be needed. The resort was as billed: huge. It was nestled near the top of the mountain and from the outside looked like something you'd see in Europe, or Colorado, certainly not Michigan.

If tourists and skiers were willing to make the trek up here, it certainly seemed like it would be worth it. I followed signs, done up in some sort of Celtic or old-world looking lettering which, despite their hint to the old world, clearly marked the route to the top.

As I got closer, I could hardly believe what they'd constructed here. The central ski lodge was stunning. It looked like a combination timber lodge, and castle rolled up into one. Everything was new -- I understood that -- but somehow it also invoked a feeling that it had been here forever. I supposed that if you were going to get people who wanted to celebrate Samhain instead of Halloween, you needed to appeal to those who knew what it was. Samhain was the precursor to Halloween. It was the ancient Gaelic festival to usher in the darker half of the year, winter. Though here, winter was way more than half the year.

I rolled up to a security guard at the entrance of the drive and pointed to the Your U.P. News placard on the dashboard.

"Marzie Nowak, here for the news conference."

"Follow the drive up, ma'am."

"Thanks."

It was amazing how the rundown Widow's Peak had been rehabbed. For years no one even knew who owned this land. I guess all that had been cleared up.

Maybe Candy Hitchcock did know what she was doing. Whoever put this place together had to have major cash and for sure had done it up right.

I parked my Jeep and walked up to the event.

Candy Hitchcock was there, standing in front of the massive entrance. She wore a lavender wool coat, which was tailored to perfection. She had a matching scarf neatly tucked into her collar and sported matching gloves. It was windy up here, but she looked impeccable.

She caught my eye and walked over.

"Marzie!" We hugged, and a whiff of her Chanel perfume reminded me that I probably smelled like crime scene and coffee.

"This is amazing, Candy," and I wasn't lying. Samhain Slopes

Resort wasn't what I had expected for a tourist attraction in little Widow's Bay.

"Oh, the owner loves the whole haunted witch thing we've got going. He's playing up that mystique." The resort, the All Souls Festival... it sure seemed well coordinated.

"And where's the owner?" I asked. I'd like to get a look at who had decided to bet a fortune on Widow's Bay.

"He's inside. He'll join us after the ribbon cutting pictures. His associates will do that with the other council members and me. He's very elusive. I just met him in person today; we'd done all the work with his people. I had no idea he was going to even make it to today's thing."

"Was it hard to get this through? I am just getting up to speed on Widow's Bay news."

"Ridge Schutte fights me on everything. He's running against me for Mayor. He thinks tourism will ruin our town. I say we need jobs. Period."

"Can I get an official interview?"

"Sure, how about right after the photo ops?"

"Sounds good."

"And I'm so glad you're back in town. We'll have to get together at Frog Toe! Tatum's turned it into a hot spot, with the festival, the fairy doors, the resort, well, it's a good time to be back in Widow's Bay."

"Fairy Doors?"

"Yes, a bunch of businesses and homes have them now. They just popped up. Fairy Door Tours-- Pauline's working on that one. You'll have to do a story!" Candy gave me a wink and another quick squeeze. She also fixed her eyes on another reporter.

"Dave Dobson," Dobson had a credential from MLive.com. I'd learned MLive was Your U.P. News' main competition. I'd crush him! Or I'd try to anyway. I looked around. There were also a few television stations here, one from Marquette and one from

The Soo. What do you know? This was a pretty big deal, apparently.

The event began, and Candy was front and center.

Several officials spoke about how the resort sported four-hundred rooms and fifty condos. The place had downhill skiing, cross-country trails, and water sports in the summer. I recorded as they talked about projections for how the place would bring in thousands of tourists and millions of dollars. I couldn't imagine a bustling Widow's Bay, but that's what they were pitching. I jotted down notes.

Outgoing mayor Paul Fisk came to the little lectern they'd set up. He'd served three terms and was retiring. For the entire time, he'd been mayor, Widow's Bay had been in economic decline, if not an emergency. Not exactly the best resume.

Candy stood by Mayor Fisk's side and looked with a smile as he spoke.

"We're confident that not only will the current businesses in Widow's Bay see a huge boost from the influx, but even now, new businesses are applying for permits, moving in, and want to grow right along with this amazing resort. Let me hand the scissors and the microphone over to the lovely councilwoman, and future mayor, we hope, Candy Hitchcock. Her work to secure the necessary permits and permissions has paved the way for the swift completion of this project."

"Thank you, Mayor Fisk, no doubt we shred the gnar on this one!"

The assembled staff behind Candy laughed. I assumed that "shred the gnar" was a ski term, but I had no idea. Candy was smooth, man, totally smooth.

She got serious, though, and started in on her official duty.

"On behalf of the citizens of Widow's Bay and the Widow's Bay Town Council, I hereby welcome Samhain Slopes Resort to our community and declare it officially open. Here's to perpetually fresh powder!"

She used a pair of big gold-plated scissors and cut the ribbon. The big wigs, hotel staff, and politicians all applauded.

"Take a look up there!" Candy pointed, and I followed her gesture. She pointed to the top of Widow's Peak, where a line of skiers appeared. They were doing the first official run down the mountain. The October snow had been perfectly timed, I guess. I had to say I was jealous. It looked fun.

"Everyone join us inside for a tour of the lodge," Candy said. I looked at the skiers for a moment, then grabbed a few pictures before I walked inside.

My eyes were drawn up to the giant beams that crossed over the enormous vaulted ceiling of the lobby. At the end of the room, a fire roared inside a fireplace big enough for fifty people to sit in. It was circular and open from all sides. It was also tall enough for a full-sized human to stand upright inside.

This was a ski resort on steroids.

"The lodge honors the history of the Upper Peninsula from First Nation people to the French trappers, and early settlers, to the miners and logging industries of the last century. And it also brings in the local Gaelic folklore of the early European settlers as well," the tour guide explained as he pointed out carvings in the wood.

I took photos, and some video as the tour continued throughout the main lodge.

"Along with full hotel accommodations here and a planned five-star restaurant, currently the property is equipped with six yurts and six cabins that can be rented for smaller parties wishing more private settings. That number will double as construction continues."

Well, there were yurts. Nothing said party like a yurt rental.

As the tour moved forward toward the rooms, I realized I was freezing from the ribbon cutting. It was now journalistically imperative that I get an up-close look at the entire fireplace. The stones of the chimney went up through the vaulted ceiling. I'd catch up with the tour in a moment once I could feel my feet.

I walked around to the far side of the fireplace and looked up in awe as the flames warmed me.

I nearly fell over when I realized I wasn't alone.

"It looks like you lost your tour." A man was sitting by the fire. I hadn't seen him when we entered. His long legs were stretched out in front of him. His leather cowboy boots were propped on the hearth. He wore a crisp white shirt, and his hair was nearly as white as the shirt, and it fell just past his shoulders.

He looked at me with ice-blue eyes and with a hint of amusement.

"Excuse me, yeah, I needed a hit of this massive fireplace."

"Impressive, no?" The man had a slight accent. I would guess French.

"I'm Marzie Nowak, reporter for Your U.P. News." The man looked me up and down. It was a bit unsettling. I found myself hoping I didn't have lettuce in my teeth and wishing I'd have done a little more than the jeans and turtleneck I'd been so satisfied with this morning. Agnes the Cat had warned me I looked frumpy next to this crisp piece of work. Maybe I'd ditched my fancy clothes too soon!

The man stood up. And up. He towered over me. He walked forward. His motions were smooth but strangely quick.

"Hello Marzenna, I'm Stephen Brule, I own the place." He was a wealthy French guy. Not too many of those were lurking around my beat in Detroit. I put out my hand, and he took it in his.

Instead of a handshake, he lifted it to his lips and kissed it! I was in too much shock to react quickly enough to stop it. What the hell, buddy?

"Uh, whoa there, this is Michigan, we do handshakes. And how did you know Marzenna was my name?"

"Pity. And Marzie isn't a proper name at all. That is obvious." I shook my head and decided to take the opportunity to at least get an interview. Stephen Brule was handsome, slick, and clearly used to wooing the ladies. Whatever, I had questions, and it looked like at this moment, I had an exclusive. The rest of the reporters were dutifully on the tour.

"So how much did this project cost?"

"Money, it's so unseemly to discuss."

"Just getting the facts for my story."

"Since I'm a private entity, I'm in no way required to give you a figure."

"So, over ten million?" Mr. Brule rolled his eyes.

"More? Over fifty million."

"Closer, but that isn't the point of your story, is it, because it would be so boring. You don't seem boring."

"Oh, I assure you, I'm boring." Mr. Stephen Brule was talking in double entendres. I was entendre impaired. The last time I'd flirted on purpose was decades ago, and I'd wound up accidentally pregnant and married half a second later.

"I doubt that."

"So, what story do you want to be told about Samhain Slopes Ski Resort?"

Stephen Brule thought about the question for a second, and then his deep voice gave me the official answer.

"Jobs, vital here in Michigan, as I'm sure you're aware. The resort will employ two-hundred from housekeeping to ski instructors, to managers, to waitstaff, to security."

"Yes, but aren't those jobs part-time, seasonal, and well, let's be honest, not living wage?"

"Not at all. Full-time for most, and year-round. They are good wages and benefits. We plan to be open for all the water sports, hiking, and what do they call it repelling? We will also have some seasonal, but I believe the region needs career opportunity, so that's what we've created." I started thinking maybe my sons should apply for next summer because it sounded like a great gig.

"And Candy Hitchcock, the Mayor says she was a lynchpin in getting this done?"

"She worked with my associates quite a bit, I hear. Though this is my first chance to meet her. I must say between her, and now you, I'm quite impressed with the beauty here at Widow's Bay."

"Slow your roll, buddy. Does that work with European women?"

"Yes." He smiled, and I had to admit I was disarmed. Stephen Brule may be an incorrigible flirt, but he was also ridiculously charming.

"Are you booked yet?"

"No, I am available for drinks and dinner."

"Uh, no, the resort."

"Pity. I am told we're filling up fast here."

"One more thing, as a favor since I've put up with your shameless flirting. How about you not talk to all the other journalists here today?"

"I believe the idea for the day was to get publicity for the resort. How would that help?"

"They'll all do the story, they'll all have the pictures, and the facts, and even interviews with your PR people. The resort will get plenty of publicity."

"And you'll have the exclusive with the owner."

"I just started at Your U.P. News. If I give them an exclusive with the elusive owner of the Samhain Resort, I look good to my boss."

"I don't think you need my help to look good to anyone, but I hate the press, so I will disappear and let you have the exclusive."

"Ugh, that was a groaner," I said and shook my head, "Oh, one more thing: why Samhain?"

"It's always best to cultivate your roots, not run from them. This place has deep roots with witches, magic, myth. Part of the appeal."

"Uh, or why people stay away," I replied but jotted down the information.

"I better make myself scarce, or your exclusive will be at risk. It was a pleasure to meet you, Marzenna." This time Stephen Brule offered a bow.

"Just let me get a quick picture for the story..."

I looked down at my phone and unlocked the camera feature.

I looked up, and the man was gone.

"Mr. Brule?"

I looked around the massive fireplace, peered around the hall, but he'd disappeared.

I guessed elusive was right.

I suppressed a smile; I didn't want my competition to know that I got an interview they wouldn't. I made a mental note to find out more about the outrageous flirt who, by more than his account, would help turn Widow's Bay economy around.

I had what I needed from this news event. I made one final call on my way back to the office to file the second story of the day.

"Ridge Schutte, please."

Schutte, Candy's rival for Widow's Bay's top job, wasn't at the ribbon-cutting for a reason.

I introduced myself and asked for a response to the opening of Samhain Slopes Resort.

His reaction was adverse, vehement, and predictable. He was the opposite of Candy Hitchcock on what was right for Widow's Bay.

"Tourists, traffic, foreign money? Is that what we want for our town? The labor will be cheap, and the shot to the economy will be temporary. Not to mention crime! We're opening the door to God knows what with this place. We need industry here in Widow's Bay, the right industry, not entertainment."

"Thank you, Councilman Schutte."

We ended the call. I drove back to the office with a good handle on what I'd write for Your U.P. News.

I typed up my story with the headline promoting my exclusive with Brule and the interview with the opposition. I sent it to Justin. I hoped he would like it. I may have been a news anchor, which to some means talking head, but I was a reporter at heart, always, and I wanted my new newsroom to see I had chops.

A few minutes later, my phone buzzed.

"Nice work! We've been trying to get Stephen Brule on the record for two years. No one has ever seen him."

"Yeah, well, he slipped away before I could get a picture, but otherwise, we're good?"

"A murder, an exclusive, and a little controversy out in sleepy old Widow's Bay, yeah, I'd say we're good. Can't wait to see what you stir up tomorrow."

"Thanks, talk to you then."

Day one of my new life was in the books. Now it was time to rekindle old friendships.

And have a beer.

CHAPTER 5

The Frog Toe was going gangbusters, and it wasn't even eight o'clock yet. But luckily, I was friends with the owner.

Tatum McGowan and her husband Pat ran The Frog Toe. It used to be called McGowan's. It was always a fun place to kick back after work. But after Pat McGowan died, and yes -- it was the bus crash -- Tatum had taken charge.

She changed the name, right in line with the new emphasis on ghosts, souls, and magic, and in the process transformed it into a hot spot. Tatum's microbrews were becoming legendary for their taste and their, uh, effectiveness. People believed that brews from Frog Toe had unique properties. Tatum wasn't doing anything to change that perception.

The Frog Toe had a big boiling cauldron suspended over a fire tucked in one corner of the big tavern-style building. The cauldron was another play on the fact that Widow's Bay was the setting for a million ghost stories about magic, monsters, and even witches. I still had a hard time getting used to it. All of a sudden, we weren't embarrassed by the bad luck and odd superstitions of Widow's Bay? I was stuck in the old perception, I guess. I tried to downplay it for years when I was in Detroit.

The Upper Peninsula was mysterious and remote to the rest of the country, heck to most of Michigan. Tall tales had a way of getting bigger here, everything was big here. And in my fact-driven life, the reputation of my hometown was a joke at best, an embarrassment at worst.

But Tatum predicted the tourists and college kids would love the cauldron. She played up the mythology instead of poo-pooing it. She was right. Customers were spreading the word that the names on the craft beer menu were effective spells, not just cute titles.

The thing was, Tatum and a lot of the women of Widow's Bay, well, maybe we did have something extra. Nothing as exciting as witch powers, but I was pretty sure I caused the cold sore on Sam's face the day I caught him cheating with Kayleigh. And Kayleigh literally did fall backward when I pushed the force of my anger towards her.

And that wasn't the first time my will had turned into reality. But I tried not to think about that.

Tatum's talents were different. She could brew up what you needed.

Her current best seller in the bar was Love at First Flight. The gimmick? If you shared a flight of Tatum's concoctions with your date, in equal measure, you'd fall in love with each other by the last sip.

"Your customers act like they never heard the term beer goggles before," I argued when I'd seen how many people were buying up what Tatum was selling.

"True, but I've got a business to run," Tatum was going to ride the wave of the popularity of microbrews as long as she could. Who could blame her? She was a single woman of a certain age, just like I was now, and we had to be badass to survive.

"Look, this stuff is more than just a love potion," she relayed a story to me about what happened right after the Charity Bus Tragedy.

One of the widows, the mom of the football team's center, Big Bonnie, was in trouble financially. Her husband, Dale, didn't have insurance, and he'd taken out loans on their business. Their business was the only strip club in Chippewa County, but hey, hunters need something to do when the sun went down.

Tatum conjured up a special brew in Bonnie's honor, hoping the money would find her and help with their debts. Sure enough, Big Bonnie was at Dondee Lanes in The Soo, meeting relatives and planning the wake for Dale, and not twenty-four hours after Tatum made a special brew for Bonnie, she went on a Keno winning streak. She walked out of the bowling alley with enough winnings to pay her business debt and an upgrade to a fancy headstone for Dale.

That's the legend of how Hot Keno Stout was born. Reports from as far downstate as Flint were coming in about little windfalls after drinking a Frog Toe Hot Keno Stout.

If the way her business boomed was magical, the way she ran the joint was practical. Tatum was tough and efficient.

I made my way to the cauldron and caught Tatum's eye.

"Welcome home!" She met me there, enfolded me in a hug, and put a bottle in my hand.

"Thank you. This place is nuts."

"I know. Not only are we overrun with Hoopsters, but I've also got the locals, and an influx of handsome, rugged types. Must be a full moon. The girls saved you a space."

A gigantic man with a beard that was bushy enough to hide another human person tapped Tatum on the shoulder.

"Can we get a round over here," the burly bushy man asked.

"Yea, hold on. Head over to the girls, and I'll pop in when it calms down. If it calms down." Tatum was tiny, fierce, and she handled a lot of boisterous patrons, but from the looks of things, Tatum was going to have to hire a bouncer or two. Heck maybe even add on to the place if it was going to continue to burst like this on a Tuesday night.

I scooched through the crowd, careful not to spill my beer. As I got closer to the cauldron, I was enveloped in more hugs.

Tatum had called in Fawn Campana and Georgie Parris. The four of us in one combination or another had been best friends since kindergarten.

"Welcome home!" They both looked spectacular to me. Fawn's high cheekbones and long dark hair hadn't changed a bit, and Georgie was the complete opposite with freckled skin and auburn locks. Seeing both of them and Tatum was the tonic I needed.

"You look like you've lost two-hundred pounds," Georgie said, and we all settled into seats around the fire.

"More like a one-hundred-eighty-pound anchor weighing me down. And get this Sam recently got into Paleo and lost twenty pounds. Keeping in shape for your girlfriend is work, you know."

"What a fool. But we get you back, so we should thank him," Fawn said.

Just like Tatum, Fawn and Georgie were fixtures of Widow's Bay. Fawn was the town veterinarian, and Georgie owned a bookstore slash deer processing establishment.

The bookstore was her idea, and the deer processing was her late husband's. The Broken Spine was a compromise that kept a steady though continually shifting clientele through Georgie's doors.

And of course, they were now widows.

"Maybe the universe conspired to put us all back together when we need it the most?" Fawn was a scientist and the daughter of one of the elders of the Ojibwa tribes. She had no doubt that the mystical and the scientific existed in tandem. Fate and quick legal settlements could work together with no problem in her worldview.

Whatever the reason, the fact remained I was here with my oldest and dearest friends. And the beer was cold.

"We heard day one was a doozy. Old Lottie Bradbury, eh?" Georgie said.

"I wonder if anyone found her old cat," Fawn said.

"I heard one of the Distinguished Ladies was looking for it," I remembered Maxine Proctor mentioning the cat, along with her other odd commentary.

"Any suspects?" Georgie asked.

I shook my head. "Not that police would name anyway." The morning seemed a long time ago, the day had been so packed.

"And then, I met the strangest man today at the ribbon-cutting for the new Samhain Slopes Resort."

"That looks so cool. It's going to be good for business," Georgie said.

"Were you swamped today? I mean, the town's animals are losing their collective minds today," Fawn asked Georgie, and Georgie nodded while taking a pull from her beer.

"This place, the bookstore, your clinic, a murder, an encounter with a handsome billionaire... I thought moving back to Widow's Bay would mean a slower pace." That was one-hundred percent true. I hadn't stopped going since before the sun rose.

"Nope, we're moving just as fast as Detroit, sister. We just have more layers on when we do it. Just wait until the big festival. Now about this handsome billionaire?" Georgie said.

And before I could elaborate on Stephen Brule, the sound of shattered glass had us all looking around to find the source.

A group of men who looked too hairy to be college boys and too brawny to be hip was squaring off against another group of men.

"What the heck is happening?" Fawn said, and we linked arms to try to avoid flying bottles.

"I have no idea. Frog Toe is out of control," Georgie said.

"There are zero restrictions in this town, we all have a right!" I heard one of the less hairy dudes say. The room appeared to be separating into two factions. One faction that didn't seem to know what a Gillette Razor was eyed up another group groomed to within an inch of their lives.

"Fawn, Georgie, Marzie!" Tatum was waiving us to the bar. Taking cover wasn't a bad idea. We made our way through flying fists and fleeing guests to Tatum, who was searching for something under the bar top.

"Where the hell is my shotgun?" She wasn't really asking us. I debated warning her that a shotgun blast wasn't the best course of action, but it was too late. She was rooting around farther down the length of the bar and wouldn't hear me if I had a bullhorn. A bullhorn wouldn't be a bad idea right now, actually.

"You're going to pay for that chair!" Tatum yelled as a wooden chair missed a skull and hit the brass bar rail and splintered into a hundred pieces. Tatum was fighting a losing battle with her warnings as the fists and the tables were flying.

A spray of beer dumped on our heads.

"Ah, hell no, now my beachy waves are totally messed up," Georgie said.

"We need to lock hands and get low," Fawn said. None of us argued.

We didn't question it. I grabbed Fawn's hand, and Fawn grabbed Georgie's hand.

"This needs to settle down, or Tatum's place is going to be ripped to shreds," I said. And it was true. In seconds, a boisterous crowd of customers had turned into a table-flipping melee straight out of a movie saloon brawl. I knew something had to be done, or the place would be destroyed. I could only think of all the work Tatum had done to make this place happen.

We closed our eyes. I found myself thinking the word stop, over and over again, just like I knew without knowing that Agnes the Cat was talking to me, I knew Georgie and Fawn were thinking the same thing.

A frisson of energy pulsed between our hands. I knew what this was even if I didn't want to admit I did. Our connection, our power, it was something I usually hid from even myself. But this was needed. It was an emergency. I suppressed my natural fear of it, and we pushed our will into the room.

Suddenly everything was quiet. Strangely, unnaturally quiet.

The three of us slowly stood up. Tatum walked toward us. But none of us could take our eyes off what we were seeing.

The entire bar was frozen in time, except the four of us. The lumberjack looking dudes were mid-swing, a beer bottle aimed for a head stopped in midair with droplets of ale suspended like amber baubles.

"We're all seeing this, right?" I asked. They nodded.

"Did we just do this?" Georgie asked. We had, probably, one way or another.

If it was a delusion, all four of us were seeing the same delusion.

I shook my head and dropped Georgie and Fawn's hand to rub my eyes. This couldn't be real. Everyone was stopped in time, even time was stopped. We stood paralyzed by what our eyes were telling our brains. That we'd frozen the hot-headed brawl by wishing into being.

Before that thought could take hold, something pressed the play button in the bar, and the fight was back on. The yelling, the music, the crashing all took right back up where it left off.

"Cease!" It was a low booming voice, and everyone in the bar stopped again. This time it wasn't some whacky freeze frame. It was real. Everyone turned to look toward who issued the actual command.

I stretched up to my tiptoes to see who was at the door. Who had yelled cease, just as forcefully as we'd thought it?

I recognized the white hair and intense blue eyes. But there was no air of amusement right now.

Stephen Brule had ordered the fight to stop.

He stood in the doorway of The Frog Toe, and his eyes scanned the patrons of the bar.

"You'll stop immediately." The crowd of people who'd just seconds ago had been ready to rip each other's throats out simmered down about one-hundred degrees from boiling.

The beer bottle that I'd seen suspended in mid-swing was in the big arm of a blonde-haired man who'd best be described as polar bear sized. He lowered it to his side without striking anything. Rightly so. It was a shame to waste a drop of a Frog Toe brew.

Stephen Brule walked further into the Frog Toe.

That's when Tatum snapped out of it.

"All of you, out, and if you can't behave, you'll be banned for life." She gripped the shotgun with her toned arms. Her jaw was set. Brule may have gotten their attention, but Tatum was going to be sure not to waste it. Banned for life was about as bad as it got for Frog Toe patrons.

Beer and stupid were a predictable combination. To keep people on their toes, if they got too stupid, Tatum had a White Board of Shame.

The board was tacked up behind the bar. On it was a list of permanently banned patrons and those who only had Frog Toe Time Outs. That list was the dreaded adult swim. If Tatum put you on the White Board of Shame, you needed to get out of the water. If you were good, maybe you would be allowed to dive back in. If you weren't, you'd be Banned for Life.

Tatum had lowered the shotgun and was now brandishing her whiteboard marker. She waved it around like it was more lethal than the firearm.

"That's right, banned!" Georgie, Fawn, and I looked at each

other. Then we watched Brule dismantle hostilities like there were pieces of an engine he was working on.

Stephen Brule circled the various contingents in the bar. He seemed to menace some individual pockets of disputes. With others, he put a hand on a shoulder or only exchanged a look.

The warring factions got a little less distinct as he circled. The men who I could only say somehow seemed more like Brule, European looking, expensive clothes, nodded to him without any other significant interaction. The other equally intimidating group was the complete opposite of the manicured menace of the first group. If Brule and his type were the French Court, this other contingent were mountain men who only recently discovered things like forks.

The rest of the bar of locals and Yoopers had settled down quickly, even though they had been swept up in the melee.

I swear as the noise level subsided, I heard random growling.

I watched as the hostile parties dispersed, went to neutral corners, and the bar resumed normal operations. The entire weird explosion couldn't have lasted much more than five minutes, but then again, we had a literal timeout, so who really knew?

Brule approached my friends and me. Seeing their jaws open in awe made me realize mine was in the same gaping position. I snapped it shut. Brule looked at me with his ice-blue eyes.

"Thank you for reaching out. We must talk later. I'll make amends with the owner of this establishment. Is it that woman? Her name?"

"Tatum, yeah, that's the one," I said, and he bowed to the three of us and floated over to the bar.

"Madame, let me help," Brule said in that courtly way that seemed out of place, heck out of century.

"What? Are you the king of the bouncers because that's what I need, mean ones."

Tatum was used to wrangling bar fights and had shaken off

the disturbance. She'd worked toward getting this place back to business as usual as fast as possible.

"Wait, was that the elusive developer of the Samhain? Your billionaire?" Georgie asked me as we watched the bar return to basically normal, if not still very crowded.

"He's handsome as hell, and what did he mean you summoned him?" Fawn said.

"I really have no idea, and he's not my billionaire."

"You know the three of us haven't done that in over twenty years. I'm not sure if I'm happy or scared that we still can," Georgie said.

"It's just like…" Fawn started the sentence, and all three of us, in unison, finished it, "Seventh Grade Field Day."

The bar fight was like seventh grade field day times ten.

CHAPTER 6

*I*t still takes three of us," I said to Georgie and Fawn.

"Yep, and it got stronger," Fawn replied.

"Yeah, Marzie's the big key there, that's our best three."

"What?" I had been gone, but they apparently had been dabbling.

"We sort of helped the football team win a state championship," Georgie admitted, and I shook my head in disgust.

"That's terrible," I said.

"Um, I seem to recall you saying Sam's reporter side piece went flying backward when you gave her the evil eye," Georgie replied.

"Yeah, well, that wasn't planned, and she deserved it."

Tatum came over after order was restored.

"That Brule guy gets the job done. He's going to send over some experienced bouncers. Says he wants the bar to be a great attraction along with his new resort. And he's going to help pay! Says it's good business for him."

Tatum's eyes lit up at the thought of getting a good deal. I think she probably was restraining herself from rubbing her hands together in glee at the offer of free help.

"He's smooth, I'll give him that," I said.

"And handsome as hell," Georgie added the obvious there.

"The three of you stopped the fight, right? I mean that's what happened, like that time you did it for field day." Tatum was witness to that one too.

"Looks like you all have been experimenting since then?"

"Hey, a winning season is good for business, too," Tatum said, shrugging off my accusatory tone.

It was a legend in Widow's Bay, the power of three. You needed three women, a clear mission, and you could get just about anything accomplished. I chose to believe that it was due to hard work and female empowered support. My friends clearly felt there was something more at work.

I flashed back to that moment in seventh grade.

The school celebrated the end of the year with a field day, where you got to wear shorts to school and ran relays outside instead of sitting in the classroom.

Shawna Leiber and Kelly Huss had words over who was "going with" Brian Shook. Words turned into hair pulling, and one hot second later, every 13-year-old in the vicinity of our playground had taken a side.

A fight broke out, and nearly two-dozen of our classmates started throwing punches and scratching.

Fawn, Georgie, and I were standing together, holding hands, and the exact same words ran through my head, stop it.

Tatum was there too, just like now, and for a brief second time froze. It was only a second or two, like tonight. But it was enough to throw ice cold water on a pack of rabid 13-year-olds.

I ran from it, literally, all the way home. And if I'm honest all the way to Detroit when I had a chance. But here it was again as soon as I moved back to Widow's Bay.

A strange power that I'd lied to myself about. A power that was stronger than that day on the playground.

Seventh grade was the last time I'd consciously used the

power of three, or whatever it was, until just a moment ago. And I hadn't meant to either time.

But it appeared that my friends had been helping their kids win football championships.

God knows what else I missed.

"You moved away. We needed a third and Tatum's got free beer," Georgie said. As though altering time and the laws of physics was a casual everyday occurrence.

"We only used the Three Powers for good. All those boys got scholarships. People around here don't have Detroit anchor-woman money to pay for school," Fawn explained. Part of me wanted to put my fingers in my ears and start humming. If I thought about it, which I tried not to, I had told myself that seventh grade was a hormone infused mass hallucination. I also thought I had a chance with John Stamos back then. Delusions and puberty go hand in hand.

I let tourists pretend that our little town was magic, or haunted, but I knew that was just a tall tale. I wasn't going to fan that flame.

"Yeah, you know Candy and Pauline asked me to join with them to fix a sinkhole to close a real estate deal. But that just felt wrong. What if some nice family moves in and pow, that sucker opens up again and swallows them up? I didn't want it on my conscience." Tatum said. One of her waiters walked by and told her he was in the weeds. Tatum was back to work without any undue anxiety over supernatural powers or witchcraft. I was currently *comprised* of anxiety about supernatural powers and witchcraft.

"This is a lot, I mean, do we really have, ugh, powers? Is that what we're talking about here?" I hated the word powers. It seemed so ridiculous.

"Yep, a lot of us in town do. Welcome back to Widow's Bay, Marzie," Georgie said and took a sip of her Frog Toe Daily Brew. My friends' steady calm was contagious. They weren't going to let me lose it over whatever had just happened. Panicking about the supernatural was ridiculous!

I struggled to get back to total denial mode. It was nice and familiar in denial mode.

"I've had all I can handle for one day, it's time to call it a night." I needed the day to end, preferably on a normal note.

"Agree, I've got a ton of appointments tomorrow," Fawn said. Her vet clinic opened early.

The three of us said our goodbyes.

So much had happened today my brain didn't know what piece of it to land on, so I turned on the 90s channel and listened to Nirvana.

A little headbanging grunge to clear my head was just the ticket. I made the quick trip home in the space of one song.

I tripped on my way into the house.

I wasn't used to its angles in the dark yet.

The haughty kitty and her manservant lifted their eyes to be sure it was me who'd interrupted their peaceful sleep. Then they both nuzzled back down into their shared pile of fluff on the dining room floor.

Other than my two symbiotic housemates, the house was quiet. I needed some quiet.

I checked their food and water and noted that I needed to get more food soon. I had traveled light, and Bubba Smith ate a lot.

I double-checked that everything was locked up tight and headed to bed. I needed sleep. I wanted sleep, a lot of it.

But I didn't hold out any hope that I'd be satisfied on that front.

There's a season in a woman's life where she sleeps peacefully and as long as she requires. I imagined Elizabeth Taylor, or maybe a Kardashian sleeps in this manner. Or a teenager, but for most women, the season of restful sleep is so brief that it's like a unicorn.

For me, motherhood was the death of sleep.

From a twin pregnancy where my bladder was some sort of trampoline to infant feedings to teenagers driving, I had lost the required biological ability to have a peaceful sleep.

I had hoped that when the twins went to college, I'd find that unicorn again. I fantasized about a blissful six or seven hours at a stretch without listening for fussy babies, or sirens, or refrigerator raids. But instead, I found perimenopause, the glittery, rainbow-filled pre-show to menopause.

Where was the Pinterest board for that, come to think of it?

Like most everything in my life, this phase came early. I was a mother, at 20, and now, not yet 40, and I was headed for "The Change." Which sounded ominous as hell and already required more plucking than a human could do in a lifetime.

A clock inside me ticked faster than it did in other people. I was accidentally overwound. I had sprung ahead without my consent.

Or, as my gyno so colorfully described, "Your eggs are rotten."

"Isn't that a bit early?"

"No, it can start as early as 35."

"So, I'll be done with it early?"

"Not necessarily, the whole thing could last well into your fifties."

My gyno didn't believe in sugar-coating the situation.

I put on my sexiest nightie, which was a Detroit Lions T-shirt that served as the only lingerie I owned and climbed into bed.

I blamed Sam's philandering for the end of our marriage, but I admit that my nightwear was on the opposite end of the sexy spectrum. So there, Sam, I'll give you that.

Agnes came in to check on me. Agnes, for all her judgment, did seem to want to be sure I was settled before she herself returned to dreamland, where she presumably was a judge on America's Top Model.

"All tucked in Agnes, go to sleep." Agnes sniffed without

conveying a pronouncement on the state of my hair or gnarly t-shirt. It was the cat's version of nurturing, I guess.

Despite the crazy day, I was an optimist that sleep could be had.

Maybe this night, I'd corral the elusive Sleep Unicorn.

I closed my eyes and did my best not to hover too long over any aspect of this packed day.

And I drifted off, in my new bed, in my old house. The last place I'd lived where sleep came in nice long stretches.

Ah, Sleep Unicorn, I've missed you so...

Unfortunately, a few hours later, the Hot Flash Squirrel landed on my chest and woke me up. The Sleep Unicorn was elusive, the Hot Flash Squirrel was not. It was everywhere, scampering in and out at will, and often.

The heat in my bed was unbearable.

I sat up and reached for the night table and my water glass.

Empty.

I got up and shuffled to the bathroom to fill it. My shin hit a box I needed to unpack. I had so much to do, I needed to try to catch a few more hours of rest.

My bedroom window faced the backyard. I'd left the blinds open.

The neighborhood backed up to a wooded area; there wasn't a reason really to worry about closing them.

I noticed something glowing in the distance.

I stepped forward and focused on the backyard. It was my backyard, and yet it wasn't.

I closed my eyes and opened them again. The blue-hued glow was still there. So was something else.

It slowly came into focus, a fuzzy focus as I blinked my eyes.

I watched as three women, in long dark dresses and strange bonnets, stood in a circle.

A tall man was in the center, his back to me. I could see he was head and shoulders taller than the women and broad through the shoulders.

He had his hand outstretched and was slowly turning to each woman, touching their foreheads.

The man wore a fur coat. Who wears a fur coat? Besides Rod Stewart? PETA protests had clearly not made their way to the Great White North.

Fog rose from the snowy ground and hovered at the knees of the people involved in the strange little scene.

I couldn't look away. They were singing a song that felt familiar though I couldn't make out a single word.

I struggled to figure out who these people were. I was born and raised in Widow's Bay. Despite leaving, I still knew just about everyone in town, yet I couldn't place a single face.

And at the same time, there was something familiar, this felt almost like déjà vu.

The man had a cap on -- coonskin, like in drawings I'd seen of Danielle Boone.

His hair was tied at the base of his neck, and slowly he rotated toward my window. I held my breath. I was going to be able to see his face if he turned just a little more.

Was this some sort of midnight re-enactment practice no one told me about from the Chippewa County Historical Society? It was the only explanation I could come up with for their strange dress. But why at night? And why in my damn backyard? Maybe they always did it, and I was the intruder?

The man rotated again and was now facing the house.

I wanted to dive down below the window and close the blinds, but it was too late.

He made eye contact with me.

I mean, I think that was impossible, right? I was in a dark room, no lights, and behind a window.

What I was seeing couldn't be real. It had to be a dream. Except it wasn't. And I knew exactly who the man was.

It was Stephen Brule. Or maybe his son? It looked exactly like him except for the outfit.

If it was Brule, gone were the bespoke custom shirts and the meticulously tailored jacket, replaced with a patchwork of furs and moccasins that came to his knees.

The rolling fog hovered low around their weird little circle.

Brule stopped staring me down and turned his focus to one of the costumed women circled around him. Now the woman turned to look at me.

The whole scene had played out with no sound, in some sort of slow motion. She saw me too! The woman who now held my gaze pointed at me. I heard her say as if it was in my ear.

"Step up."

What the heck? That was enough. I broke eye contact. I hunched down to the carpet of my bedroom floor. Then I scooted over on my butt to the cord that controlled the window blinds. I should be closing them anyway. Standing in front of a window with my t-shirt and underwear was a dumb move.

I slowly pulled the cord, and the blinds descended. Nope. I didn't see anything, and THEY didn't see anything. Time for me to get into my canoe and paddle up Denial River again!

I took a breath. Was hallucinating a part of perimenopause? I mean, no one warned me about the chin hair, maybe this was the same thing. *Yeah, you'll start seeing ghosts. The spirits will go away in ten years when you're done with the change. Also, you'll gain weight.*

I climbed back in bed.

The woman had said, step up. Just like Maxine had said to me the other day. What was up in this town?

I struggled to make sense of what I saw. It was a dream, it had to be a dream. Sleep then pulled me like the fog that was at their feet. Down. And away from the million things that were too crazy to consider.

I sunk back into sleep. But it was a strange sleep. My dreams stayed weird and vivid.

I slept in fits. I dreamed of a fort, a fire, and struggled in my dreams to try to talk. I wanted to say something. To be heard. To ask what they meant by step up?

I know I tossed and turned, but never completely woke up again until I did.

I managed to actually yell.

I think I yelled Brule in my dream. But in my bedroom, in the real world, I knew it came out as a grunt. It was no word whatsoever, and it was loud enough to wake me up.

I sat up in bed. I looked at my phone and saw that it was after 5 a.m.

I was up, and I was going to stay up. It was useless to fight it anymore, and it was best to shake off my night of weird dreams or menopause induced hallucinations or whatever. Maybe Tatum slipped me a brew she hadn't quite tested yet.

Agnes was at my bedroom door again. She looked perturbed to be so rudely awakened.

"Sorry I interrupted your beauty sleep." Agnes looked at me imperiously, affronted by my inarticulate sleep grunt.

Keep it down.

"I'll try." Geez, I was answering my cat again. I realized this was just as weird as the nighttime visions.

"I'm losing my mind, Agnes. Get used to it."

You need to exfoliate.

Great, now Agnes weighed in on skincare.

I shuffled to the bathroom and looked in the mirror for a beat.

A younger woman looks refreshed after a night's sleep. I looked the opposite. Was unfreshed a thing? That was the look I sported, unfresh.

I noticed that my pillow had made extra wrinkles on my face. Lovely.

I'd read a satin pillow could help; I'd have to order one. I was pretty sure Widow's Bay wasn't the place to purchase luxury bedding. Or maybe it was. Widow's Bay was nothing if not surprising these days.

I brushed my teeth and assessed again as my eyes adjusted.

I had good hair, I owned that. It fell in thick waves around my face and skimmed my shoulders. But it needed a rest. I'd forced it into tv lady submission with spray and heat for too long. And I'd dyed the hell out of it to keep ahead of the gray. Hiding gray was the last of my worries the past few days. Despite those grays, I knew I wasn't old enough to be losing my marbles like this.

I'd suspected dementia in Maxine and Elsie, and yet I was the one seeing a Mayflower style rager in my backyard in the middle of the night. I was talking to cats and casting time spells at the microbrewery.

Welcome home, indeed.

I thought about my dream again. It had to be a dream.

"Marzie, you were dreaming. Rod Stewart is not holding a séance underneath the backyard swing set." Saying it out loud made whatever happened last night, even nuttier.

Don't forget to buy Bubba Smith his food.

I jumped a foot, Agnes, of course.

"I'm going to class."

Nothing ever got worse because you worked out.

Maybe intentional sweating was what I needed instead of the hostage style sweating of a hot flash.

I also needed real live people, not snarky cats, or haunted dreams.

I grabbed a water bottle and headed to Pauline's class.

CHAPTER 7

On the way to Pauline's class, I estimated that I'd had less than three hours of actual sleep the night before.

I drove the few blocks into town. It was before six, and the sky was still dark.

October in the U.P. meant you drove to work in the dark, and you drove home in the dark. And when there was sun in the winter, we did not take it for granted. When it showed up, it was worshipped in all its brilliance.

Samhain Slopes and Widow's Bay planners were already looking at a Summer Solstice Fest if this All Souls thing next week worked out. Revelers could enjoy surf, sun, and sand that was salt and shark-free. Throw in a little dancing around the May Pole, and you could sell t-shirts about the experience.

Widow's Bay was a small town, and by Michigan standards, heck by North American standards, it was ancient. Maybe the play to tap into ancient myth was a good one. Or maybe it would fall flat on its Celtic Knot.

The snow had blown off the road but stuck lightly everywhere else. And more was on the way. My Jeep dipped down fast and hard into a pothole.

"Oops, sorry. Didn't see that one coming." I apologized to my Jeep. When the potholes got deep around here, cobblestone from centuries past peeked through.

People that lived in the U.P. were a bit of an oddity, even to other Michiganders, I'd learned from my time downstate. They were an eclectic mix of people with only a few things in common. They were willing to live at the tip of the country, in rugged conditions, they were unfazed by cold, and they didn't let one second of the incredible burst of summer that came in July and left in August go to waste.

I grew up appreciating the gigantic cold beauty that was still untamed in the U.P. It was easy to forget, living in Suburban Detroit, that the wild, untamed north was a highway drive away. I didn't see a single car on my trip into town. It was so different than the commute I'd had to the station over the years. And as that thought flitted across my mind, the traffic picked up. It wasn't, however, traffic from other vehicles.

I slammed on my brakes when a dark shadow jutted out from the trees and into the road. My headlights caught a furry, four-legged dog run across the road. And then another one.

But they weren't dogs, it had to be-- were they wolves?

Wolves weren't common in Northern Michigan; I mean, they were here. I thought the Michigan DNR estimated that there were under a thousand. I'd never seen one, and yet here were two, crossing the road! And these two were huge, one was black, and one was red.

They didn't pay my Jeep any attention and dashed into the thick tree line again.

I was amazed and wondered if that was a story? Were wolves making a comeback up here? Moose yes, coyotes yes, even bears, but wolves? I made a mental note. I needed to brush up on my Department of Natural Resources contacts for future story ideas.

It was amazing, really, to encounter gigantic wolves on your morning commute. I put my foot on the gas, slowly. Everything was bigger here, I had forgotten that, even the animals.

The closest "big city" to Widow's Bay was Sault Ste. Marie, The Soo, and a fair number of people from Widow's Bay commuted there to work. Depending on the weather it could take thirty minutes, or it could take two hours.

Not many people commuted into Widow's Bay, so I supposed that was the reason I had the roads to myself this morning. Most families in Widow's Bay had at least one four-wheel-drive vehicle, a snowmobile, and a boat. I had wondered about snowmobiling around town, but seeing the wolves made me realize I wasn't at that level of self-sufficient. The Jeep would do just fine.

My drive took under ten minutes, and I was in the heart of town, more signs were going up that the big festival was close. I parked at the Old School House Commons for Pauline's class. I hoped I could make this a routine exercise. I had failed at that when I was a working mommy.

Pauline had never failed at work and working out. Pauline's passions were real estate and fitness.

Pauline's passion for fitness translated into torture, at least three mornings a week, with her fitness class.

Pauline was always bringing the latest fitness trend to the ladies of Widow's Bay. Currently, it was all about indoor cycling. While the big city had Soul Cycle franchises, Pauline was rocking her own thing. She told me it was Soul Cycle adjacent, Snow Cycle.

I hoped I could keep up. Pauline was as fit as a woman could be in my estimation. She had Michele Obama arms for Pete's sake.

I walked in and spied my crew in the back row, thank God. I didn't want to be in the front.

Georgie and Fawn were adjusting their bike seats. Candy Hitchcock was also there and, no surprise rocked matching leggings and workout tank. I regretted my black bike shorts and generic gray t-shirt, but then Georgie and Fawn were similarly underwhelming in the workout gear department.

"Morning, ladies. No Tatum?"

"No way, she stays up too late at the bar to make this class or any class," Fawn said.

"And yet she remains buff, that's not fair." I had to literally eat nothing to hold steady. Though eating nothing only worked when your life was in full upside-down mode.

"It's lifting those kegs," Georgie said, and we all slowly started pedaling our bikes to nowhere.

There were about a dozen of us in the studio, and Pauline had the lights low, but her energy, as usual, was high.

"We're going to be on a ride in the Italian Alps." The impossibly fit Pauline had a microphone headset on. Music blared, as she tried to set the scene to maybe make us forget how much we were about to sweat or that we were not in the frigging Italian Alps.

"What was I thinking? Why am I doing this again?" Georgie asked no one in particular.

"Got me," I said as Pauline prompted the class to increase the resistance on our bikes and warm up!

"Well, this week is better than last week. My lady parts are less, uh, bruised. I think I'm getting used to it?" Candy said, trying to offer a bright side.

"Lady parts," Fawn rolled her eyes at Candy's description.

"I hear they have some sort of padded shorts you can wear," Georgie said.

"We're here to get rid of padding, I'm not going to add any," I said between panting breaths. Talking was getting to be a challenge.

"Agree. I'm worried my thighs are getting bigger from all this biking. I don't want my thighs bigger," Candy looked at her legs as they pumped up and down to the music.

"Candy, the only big thing on you, is your hair," Georgie said, and I laughed despite myself. I had some majorly big anchor hair in my day too.

We were just getting into the warm-up part of the class when something which could only be described as unprecedented happened. A man walked in.

Calling what walked in a man was an understatement. A tall, muscular, auburn-haired man with an actual man bun walked into class and picked out a bike.

He draped a towel over it and started pedaling. He was taking the class like it was totally normal. My girlfriends looked at each other, rather wide-eyed. A man in a class at the Y was no biggie in the big city, but here, no, not so much. Men in Widow's Bay didn't do boutique fitness like they didn't do fat-free cheese.

"His hair's better than Fawn's," Georgie whispered to me, and it was true. Fawn had gorgeous long thick locks, but our new classmate could give her run for her money with his thick auburn man bun.

We continued to pedal and follow Pauline's cues. But the focus was now on our unexpected new classmate. Despite the muscled physique and the hipster hair, our new classmate didn't look like a college kid. He had a few crow's feet, a bit of tarnish on his tan skin. Not that I was obsessing or anything.

"Turn up the tension, crank that knob to the right! We're almost to the top of the first hill!" We followed Pauline's instructions, and our male classmate seemed not to notice us noticing.

"You crank that nob," Georgie said, and I bit my lower lip.

"I wonder if it's all-natural or if he has those padded shorts," Fawn said. I tried not to laugh. I also felt a little spike of joy. These women really were what I needed after the month I'd had. They made me laugh, they picked me up, and we really could say anything to each other.

"Are these bike seats heated like my car for crying out loud," Georgie added, and it was the last straw, I couldn't hold back the giggling.

"You're grown women, get a grip." Candy struggled to rein us in and establish some semblance of decorum. It was in vain.

We spent more time goofing around in the back row than pedaling up the fictional mountain, but it somehow made the 45-minute class go by faster.

Finally, Pauline was telling us to inhale, stretch our arms, and high five the biker next to us.

"You did it! You left your weaker self behind you, ladies. And gentleman! Turn that nob to the left, release that tension! It's all downhill from here."

The class finished, and the man who'd been all the buzz turned and smiled at the sweaty back row.

"Good class, my name's Grady," he said to us. I noticed a twinkle in his amber eyes as he introduced himself. No doubt he'd heard us cackling up a storm. We were now at a loss for words. Grady draped the towel over one well-defined shoulder and walked out.

"Wow. That's a first!" Pauline came over to the women.

"I don't think you've ever had a man within fifty-feet of one of your classes," said Georgie as she mopped sweat off her red curls.

"What's going on here? You all have been telling me that there was a shortage of men around here. They're everywhere!" It was true. They'd all complained to me at one point or another that the dating pool for a woman in her late thirties in Widow's Bay was shallow as a goldfish bowl.

"He's probably one of the new loggers," Candy said.

"How are you not drenched in sweat," Fawn asked Candy, and she waved off the question.

"Loggers, there hasn't been logging here in our lifetimes." The Upper Peninsula had been nearly completely deforested in the last century but thanks to regulations and the industry totally collapsing over the decades, the entire region was lush and dense with mature trees.

Widow's Bay was once also home to copper mining back in

the day, but that day was long ago, and the economy here was anemic.

However, thanks in large part to Candy's marketing of the town and Pauline's real estate acumen, Widow's Bay was on the cusp of economic progress and redevelopment. A fact Candy mentioned in all her speeches. Bringing logging and or mining back to the area was actually the focus of my story that last day at WXYD.

It was amazing really that the economy in Michigan could finally be on the uptick.

"Look, this class isn't the only place I work my butt off." I had to give it to Candy, she was a force of nature.

"And that damn Ridge Schutte has been fighting me every step of the way. He's all for mining but wants to stop logging and tourism. Anything I do, he wants the opposite."

"Let's go over and get some coffee to go, then I have to get to work," Fawn said, interrupting Candy's complaints. I suspected they'd heard it a million times.

We headed out of the Old Post Commons and walked along Main to grab a morning coffee.

The cold air felt good on my skin as we walked. Pauline's class was no joke, I had worked up a good sweat even though I'd giggled through most of it.

I made sure to walk with Candy. If I was going to be a reporter in Widow's Bay, I needed to know what was what, from murders to church picnics, to economic development, to politics, and Candy was the best source.

"So, you said Ridge is blocking progress?"

"Ridge is blocking a key permit we need for the loggers. I've had a million phone calls with the new owner of the mine, and they're ready to get rolling. He says we are looking at over one-hundred new jobs, and that damn Ridge is fighting against it. Just like he did with the ski lodge. But permit or not it looks like from our new classmate that some of those loggers are already in town," Candy said.

"What's his main objection?"

"He hates outsiders, he hates progress, he hates me winning, or all of the above. He's got a crony who wants to do copper mining, of course, and that could be in direct opposition to the logging," Candy said.

I tried to suppress it, but while Candy described her feud with Ridge Schutte, a yawn escaped my mouth.

Fawn saw it. It wasn't because I was bored, it was because I was running on zero sleep.

"You were up dreaming last night too, I knew it. It's so weird. Last night I had the strangest dream, and the animals were ridiculously restless. Anyone else have a weird night?" Fawn lived with a menagerie of animals, and she also usually had several furry overnight patients in her clinic. And she'd caught my mid-walk yawn.

All the ladies nodded as we sipped our coffees.

"I slept like a baby." Candy was always the last to admit anything in her life was less than perfect.

"Good for you. Listen to this, in my dream that Stephen Brule, the Samhain resort man from last night, was leading some sort of duck duck goose session with a bunch of women dressed for a Thanksgiving. All of it in my backyard," saying it out loud made it even more ridiculous.

"I had a talking tree telling me to step it up," Georgie said.

"Yep, same here," Fawn said, "But in my dream, it was a dog, who talked, and told me to step up," Fawn said.

"I had a pilgrim lady in my dream, too," Pauline said. She'd caught up and was now bringing up the rear of our caffeine-fueled locomotion.

"This is new, the first time we've all had the same dream, right?" After the incident in the Frog Toe, I was starting to think anything was possible.

"Ha, except when we all dreamed John Stamos was taking us to the prom," Georgie said.

"I didn't have the dream," Candy said. She was adamant, but being adamant was a job qualification for politicians even if they were lying.

"We all had weird dreams last night, except Candy, but all the dreams had the same message, step up?" I said.

"I'm going to take it to mean it's my turn to increase my inventory! If the mill is opening, people need homes. I've got some great properties available" Pauline switched gears from fitness to strange dreams to real estate that fast.

"Step up to Superior Real Estate," Georgie said. Pauline never slowed down or ever quit.

"Yep, that had to be it. We all dreamed up a new slogan for your business cards. Tomorrow night we'll dream up a clearance sale for Georgie's shop," I said.

"Right," Georgie added.

"The real point is a man was in Pauline's class, I can't believe we're not talking about that," Candy said.

"And it looks like there's an influx of traffic up in here."

It was now seven a.m. on a Wednesday, and sure enough, there were three men, yelling at another three other men on the corner Main and Sumac Street.

"If you stay out of our zone, there's no problem," I swore I heard one of the lumberjack types growl.

"Your zone is in our territory," the two groups were squaring off. Overnight Widow's Bay had gone from a sleepy town of widows and loners in love with their snowmobiles to the Wild West. Zones? Territories? What the heck were they even fighting about?

"This is your doing, all yours, Candy Hitchcock." I whirled around behind us, and there was Ridge Schutte, angry and smug, and pointing that attitude toward Candy.

"What? People moving into town? You're right. I'll take full credit. You're welcome, Ridge, and you're welcome Widow's Bay," Candy fired back.

I honestly didn't know where to look, the fight heating up on the corner or the one in front of my face with Candy and Ridge.

"It's official, the town has gone collectively insane," Georgie said.

Georgie, Fawn, and I sunk backward and leaned on Georgie's store window.

"Is too early to pop popcorn?" Fawn quipped. She wasn't wrong. Another day another skirmish between newcomers and the old guard of Candy and Ridge. I thought I was moving back to a small quiet town. Small maybe, but nothing had been quiet since I arrived.

Candy and Ridge continued their war of words with municipal ordinance numbers flying back and forth like they were Bible verses.

"WP 121 no sign can be higher than the level of the first-floor of...." Ridge rattled something off about signage that I didn't catch. But Candy did.

"That was written before the internal combustible engine was invented Ridge, it doesn't apply," Candy said, and Pauline nodded like she was her backup, ready to throw a punch.

"Maybe I shouldn't open The Broken Spine today, with this level of crazy roaming around, someone's libel to tear my place up," Georgie said.

"Whoa," Fawn nodded her head, and we turned our attention back to the group of men exchanging words on the corner. They'd begun to push shoulders and bump chests.

"So much testosterone for this early hour," I said under my breath.

And then, in the middle of the near melee appeared my Aunt Dorothy. Her little white hair and waving finger popped up out of nowhere. Much like Pauline was backing up Candy, Elsie was little old lady back up for Aunt Dorothy.

"What is she doing?" I said, and we couldn't look away.

"You all stop it right now. Go about your business, or the pack master is going to get a call from me." What?

She was losing it. I walked forward, worried that my Great Aunt was in physical danger. Amazingly the two groups stepped away from each other. They were still eyeballing like nobody's business, but the threat of a brawl like the one that had broken out last night in the Frog Toe appeared to have passed.

The men walked away in different directions, and Aunt Dorothy with Elsie in tow spotted us, still watching in awe at the morning's skirmishes.

Candy and Ridge continued to trade insults and were oblivious to Aunt Dorothy's approach. Her wagging finger triangulated itself on Georgie, Fawn, and me.

"Did you three see that?"

"Yes, you scolded those hulks like they were four-year-olds," Georgie was impressed.

"You want to handle Candy and Ridge over there." I pointed to the political debate continuing as Candy and Pauline walked away with Ridge.

"Uh, no. Candy has plenty of magic, and so does that, Pauline. You girls need to catch up."

Girls? Magic? I did feel I needed to catch up. Dorothy was talking about something, and I had no idea what.

"I need to talk to all of you now." Aunt Dorothy was clearly worried.

"I've had enough fun for one morning. I need to get in here and get working," Georgie said.

"And I'm booked, wall to wall with patients," Fawn said. I was working up some sort of excuse as well when Elsie, ordinarily quiet, lost her cool.

"YOU NEED TO STEP UP!" She yelled it at the top of her lungs. It was the same phrase we'd all heard in our dreams. Step up. I was sure I was awake, though no amount of caffeine in the world was helping me figure out what was going down in Widow's Bay this morning.

"Shh. It's okay. They don't know yet," Aunt Dorothy put an arm around her friend.

"Okay, look, let's go in my shop," Georgie put a key in the front door and opened The Broken Spine.

"Can I get her some water?" Fawn asked as Georgie turned on some lights and pulled out a chair for Elsie and Dorothy.

"That might be good," Aunt Dorothy said.

"No, no, just get on with it, we can't do it, they HAVE to do it." Elsie wasn't making sense.

"Fine, listen, you three and the rest of your generation, you've got to understand what's happening here," Aunt Dorothy said.

"It looks like a bunch of newcomers to Widow's Bay have hot heads and don't get along," I replied. Dorothy shook her head at that.

"They belong here just as much as we do," Elsie said.

"Shh. Calm down," Dorothy said as she patted Elsie's hand.

"The gate is open, that's for sure," Elsie said.

"She's confused," Georgie replied.

"You all need to listen and learn fast. I thought we might have a little time to prepare you, but boom, they're here." Aunt Dorothy said. We were listening, but to what?

"Who's here?" Fawn asked.

"What gate?" I asked Elsie.

"She's talking about the gate that has been closed for almost two generations." Aunt Dorothy looked at all three of us.

"We did our part," Elsie said.

"Yes, we did. What do you know about the founding of Widow's Bay?" Aunt Dorothy looked at Georgie. If anyone was going to know the history of something it was Georgie, the local history section of her bookstore was better than any library's in the county.

"Some," Georgie replied.

"What I'm about to tell is buried pretty deep in our history books, but all members of the DLC know it by heart, it goes back to the trapper days before we were even a state."

"This town is important. We're important," Elsie said.

"Our ancestors made a vow, and we all have to keep that vow," Dorothy said.

"That's crazy," I said.

"Those men, they're not like other men. We finally got that gate open to let the vampires, werewolves, shifters, and the travelers back in." I was pretty sure my jaw hit the floor at that statement.

"And the trolls, don't forget the trolls, they always make such a mess," Elsie said.

"Yes, them too, Yooper Naturals, keep it lively, don't they?" And the two ladies smiled at each other. They had lost it. That was now clear. I didn't, wouldn't, indulge whatever cockamamie story they were selling.

"Okay, that's it, I'm out of here. I've got real work to do." I stood up and walked to the door.

"You can't avoid the promise. You're part of it!" Aunt Dorothy called out to me.

I left my friends and my crazy aunt at The Broken Spine.

Yooper Naturals? Vows? Gates?

It was too much, too batty, and I needed to get to work.

The best way to combat the chaos was to find something ordinary. Everything in my life was new or flipped upside down, and now this.

I struggled to stop myself from panicking.

I questioned my decision to take the job here. Was starting over back where I grew up a big mistake?

I walked out onto Main Street. Things looked normal. The regular business of life was commencing. There were no fights brewing.

I wondered if my Aunt and her friends had just collectively lost their minds.

Then there was the incident last night.

Had Georgie, Fawn, and I stopped time in the bar last night?

Or was it the beer, or some hoax?

Sure, something was happening in the town, but vampires, werewolves, shifters, and what did she say? Oh yeah, travelers.

Aunt Dorothy and her friends were unhinged.

I had work to do, real work. Work that had nothing to do with whatever nutty ideas Aunt Dorothy and Elsie had concocted.

There was a real murder, and I needed to do a follow-up.

If there was something strange in Widow's Bay, it was that an old lady was murdered, not that some monster gate was now opened.

Whatever was going on, I had a job to do. I may have a house and retirement savings covered, but to put food on the table and keep the lights on, I needed a paycheck.

I felt slightly guilty for letting Fawn and Georgie deal with Aunt Dorothy but only slightly.

The murder of Lottie Bradbury was a fact, and my job was facts.

Not a geriatric monster mash.

CHAPTER 8

A quick shower at home and a promise to pick up food for Bubba after work, and I was able to switch my focus and concentrate on my job of reporting. I had successfully climbed into a mental kayak that was crashing over a waterfall of denial without a helmet.

Of course, in twenty years, I'd never had an uneventful day of reporting. My job was to find the extraordinary. Except I'd blown a fuse on supernatural at the moment.

I just hoped for a day free of vampires, werewolves, trolls, and what else? Oh yeah, shifters.

I checked with the newsroom first.

"Yeah, do a Lottie follow up for me, and check the unusual incidents reports at the sheriff's department, and you're good to go. You know the drill, we trust you to know your community," Justin said. It was music to my ears.

I was on my way to the sheriff's office already.

"Got it. Have we done any logging stories? Or fights about re-opening mines up here?"

"We hear mining isn't happening anytime soon. But what are you hearing? More new businesses? Logging could be closer."

"Same thing. Like they might be ready to restart the logging operations up here any day now."

"Well, like I said, jobs, cats, and murder in any combination. Go get 'em."

I parked at the Widow's Bay municipal building with the hope I could get two items accomplished: a look at the unusual incident reports and an update on Lottie Bradbury's murder.

The unusual incidents reports could either be a gold mine or a snore, but you could count on a big weird crime happening the one day you didn't check. So, check, I would, every day.

It was a heck of a lot easier to get the official word on just about anything happening in Widow's Bay than it was in Detroit. The police department, the city government, the county government, and the courts were all in one convenient place, Widow's Bay Government Center. Or as the locals who weren't that keen on any government interference of any type called it, The Barrel, as in pork barrel.

It had been a while since I'd been here, but I figured I'd be stopping in daily if I stayed in Widow's Bay. The oddness of my aunt made me question the long-term viability of my plans. Had she lured me here under some idea that I could be her caregiver as she careened off the deep end? I didn't think she would do that. But maybe?

For now, though, I needed to make the sheriff's office receptionist my new best friend. If anything odd or newsworthy happened, the receptionist would be my lifeline.

Mary Jo Navarre was the woman to see. She was a year or two older than me in school.

She looked up from her desk and then looked me up and down.

"Oh my, if it isn't the big city news anchor Marzie Nowak, slumming here in Widow's Bay."

She had a snark to her. I may be born and bred in Widow's

Bay, but I left. And that was enough for a lot of people to distrust me. It looked like Mary Jo was one.

"Hardly slumming, just back home, working for the Your U.P. News."

"Up Your News, that's what Chief Marvin calls it,"

"Yeah, I've heard a few folks call it that."

Mary Jo wasn't going to be easy. But I had a plan. She had a son who played football, and I could speak football mom with the best of them, thanks to Joe and Sam Junior.

"Hey, I hear your boy is quite the lineman for the Loggers this year!"

"Oh, my yes, he's taken calls from Central Michigan, Western Michigan, all the way downstate in Adrian too. And he's only a sophomore!"

"Congratulations. From what I hear, he's going to have his pick." I knew the way to a football mom's heart if I knew anything.

"Titus will go to all the right camps this summer, and then whoever can offer the best money. You know?"

"That's right, be selective, if they want him, they can be sure to pay."

"I heard your boys play too, at MSU?"

"Oh, in high school, sure, but they were nowhere near as good as your Titus. They're not college ball level at all. I'm jealous. I miss it!" Mary Jo was now glowing. Mission Accomplished.

Now it was time to look at the log.

"Can I take a look at the unusual incident reports then?"

"Here you go," Mary Jo slid it over to me, and I gave her a grateful smile. The information was public record, but people like Mary Jo could make it easy or tough to get.

I scanned the list.

"Oh, my! A snowmobile crashed into the carryout?"

"Yep, Byron's there now, you might be able to catch him if you hurry. Hey, let him know that Todd Bialecki reported his snowmobile missing a few minutes ago. No need for Sherlock Holmes on where it wound up."

"Gotcha, I'll tell him, and Holiday Gas, that's out on Lulu Road?"

"Yep, right by the highway ramp."

"And Byron's still on the Lottie Bradbury investigation?"

"Yeah, with Bud supervising." If I hustled, I'd get two birds with one stone on this story.

"Thank you so much, and Mary Jo, if you want, I have a recipe that my sons' team loved, a dessert if you have to feed the team."

"Oh, I'd love it. Bring it by?"

"How about tomorrow morning?"

"Perfect. Nice to catch up with you Marzie, welcome back." I'd made progress with Mary Jo, which felt good and normal and not haunted or witchy. At least one thing today was.

I drove out to Holiday Gas. It looked like Loof was still interviewing employees.

I took a few pictures of the snowmobile, now lodged in the front window.

Whoever crashed probably robbed the place then took off, leaving the vehicle and the store clerks to pick up the pieces.

I left Loof to his work and checked inside.

A man was sweeping glass up off the floor. There was also a wet, muddy path leading away from the vehicle toward the counter. I took a few quick pics before anyone could tell me no.

"Hi, I'm Marzie Nowak, from Your U.P. News."

"Ah, this must be big if Up Your News is here." I could see that was going to get old, fast.

"Are you the owner?"

"Seyed Raza." He kept sweeping up.

"I wondered if you had any surveillance video of this?"

"Oh, for sure, I have cameras everywhere." He had a middle eastern accent, and I wondered about how he'd gotten to

Widow's Bay. It was always interesting to find out how people chose this place if they weren't born here.

"Mr. Raza, I can put that video up on the website, and they'll find a suspect. It works almost every time.

"Call me Seyed," Seyed continued to sweep, but the dustpan was moving around uncooperatively. I kneeled and grabbed the handle of the dustpan. Then I held it in place so Seyed could collect the shards.

"How much cash did they get?" Knocking over a gas station was still easy pickings for low-level criminals.

"Oh, that's the beauty part," Seyed answered and carefully guided the shards into the dustpan. He stood up and took it from me.

"What?"

"Come, take a look."

Seyed motioned for me to come over behind the counter. He pressed play, and four different angles of the store showed up in the monitors.

The outside camera showed a snowmobile driving up to the store and then ramming through the doors. Glass rained down, but the driver of the snowmobile seemed unharmed. He was wearing a helmet, yellow with a black stripe. It was kind of genius if you didn't want to be immediately identified. And, rather odd since he'd stolen the snowmobile from Todd Bialecki. Not many thieves think of taking safety gear as well.

The snowmobile driver got off the crashed vehicle and pulled a small handgun from his waistband. And then walked over the debris into the store. As I watched the video, Seyed moved on from broom to mop. The floor would be clean soon, even if the window would still be busted.

The overnight clerk stood perfectly still with his hands up. Good move as the snowmobile bandit pointed it right at his chest.

But instead of having the clerk open the cash drawer, the man walked around the cashier.

The helmeted robber headed to the row of cigarette boxes. He instructed the cashier to open up the lock on the plexiglass cabinet doors. The snowmobile bandit grabbed a box of cigarettes, tucked them into his coat, and walked out of the store through the broken window.

He left the snowmobile and all the cash in the drawer behind. Though he kept the helmet on.

"What the heck?"

"Totally ridiculous," Seyed said.

"He busted up your store for a pack of smokes?"

"Yep, no one hurt, no cash is gone. Oh, I do think he grabbed a Slim Jim on the way out, I need to tell the police that."

I nodded. "Smokes and a Slim Jim, that was a hell of a night," I said.

I was feeling somewhat satisfied that my instinct was right. This security video and the headline would make Justin Lamorre happy. Weird crimes were always winners, especially if a snowmobile was involved. All I needed was a cat, and it would be complete.

"A carton of smokes, Marlboro Red Label 100s actually," Seyed corrected her.

"Gotcha."

I watched as the helmeted driver walked away with the smokes in hand, and the snowmobile stuck in the window.

"Thumb drives are over there. Grab one. I'll ring it up and then copy the video for you," Seyed pointed to the electronics shelf, untouched by the recent robbery.

I paid Seyed for it and then wrestled it free from the packaging. I waited as Seyed made me a copy. I wasn't lying about finding a suspect. Usually, someone knew something, and once it was on Facebook, it was better than an all-points bulletin. Nine times out of ten, a good bit of video like this would lead to a suspect getting arrested. I was already mentally writing the head-line: *Man crashes snowmobile into gas station, swipes carton of Marl-boro Reds and beef jerky*

"Thanks, Seyed, they'll get this up by this afternoon."

"No problem."

"And here's my cell," I handed Seyed a card.

"Mega Millions gets over 30-million, or you need coverage on something text me."

"Will do."

"This will be up soon." I waved the flash drive in my hand.

Seyed nodded, and I made my way back out to Loof.

Despite the weird way the day had started, it was now moving in a solid, recognizable direction. I'd connected with two valu-able assets for any reporter. I knew the clerk at the police depart-ment and now the owner of the local convenience store.

No travelers, vamps, or trolls in sight, thank goodness.

I made a mental note to bake up something for both Mary Jo and Seyed. I could help solidify our new working relationship with a little sugar. Everyone loved fresh baked cookies, and I was going to be bugging them both for stories, well, that is if I didn't run screaming from the U.P.

"Hey, Loof." He looked to be finished with the snowmobile investigation and was walking to his cruiser.

"Yes?"

"Did anyone call Todd Bialecki? This is his snowmobile."

"What?"

"Mary Jo said he reported his missing late this morning."

"I'll be darned."

"Yep, you solved that case! Now I have a few questions on that Bradbury murder."

"I'm not authorized to talk."

"Fine, off the record then. Do you have a murder weapon?"

"No, but it was something sharp and jagged and dirty."

"Why dirty?"

"Bacterial growth on some petri dish."

I tried not to wince at the visual. "Official cause of death?"

"Trauma to the esophagus and the works in there. Officially foul play, you can say that."

"Murder."

"Yep, the first homicide in The Bay since, gosh, that time, Pam Vivanio ran over her husband with the three-wheeler on purpose."

"That was like three years ago? And no mystery on that one, right?"

"Yeah, Randy deserved worse."

"Any fingerprints, physical evidence?"

"Oh, Randy had tire tracks on his forehead, plain as day."

"No, I mean with Lottie Bradbury."

"Nothing I can tell you about."

"Okay, okay. No suspects we can report on with Lottie?"

"No."

"Any signs of forced entry to her house?"

"No. But that doesn't mean anything. She might not be the type to lock up." Loof said, but I disagreed. The kind of person who snatched fun from children's lawn toys was exactly the kind of person who always locked up. And probably didn't let people in the house all too often.

But I didn't want to tell Loof how to do his job.

"You got what you need?" Loof said as he climbed into his cruiser.

"For now," though there wasn't much to write about in the Lottie follow-up. I really needed a relative for the next story.

"Are you done at her house? I wondered if I could get a look inside, maybe get a picture for an obit?"

"Yep, that nephew of hers got the all-clear. He's probably there for whatever you need." Loof started his vehicle.

It was a great idea. At the very least, I'd learn a little about

Lottie and maybe get a better quote than, "she took my son's soccer ball."

It still wasn't noon. I checked in with Justin and let him know I'd have a snowmobile crash story, and probably a follow up to Lottie Bradbury's murder. I hoped on that second thing anyway. Loof's information was sparse, although the information about the jagged object as the murder weapon was an awful new detail I'd need to add to any ongoing coverage.

When I arrived at Lottie's house, it looked like someone was there. Maybe I'd catch a break in this story.

I knocked on the door, but there was no answer.

I knocked louder this time a man opened the door. He was long, skinny, and I'd put him in his twenties. He must be Lottie's nephew. He was probably 5'10, but if he weighed 140 pounds, I'd be surprised. He had on jeans, and his sweatshirt hung off of him.

"Hi, I'm so sorry to hear about Lottie. I'm doing a follow up for Your U.P. News. I'm a reporter, my name's Marzie. She was your aunt?"

"Yeah, it's sad." He had scraggly hair and a short, unkempt beard.

"Did you live with her?" I asked, and he shook his head no.

"No, just here cause I'm the next of kin. Haven't been to Widow's Bay in years."

"Oh, can I come in? I just have a few questions. You know, background kind of things."

"I don't really know much. She was a sweet old lady, that's all it's just terrible." First of all, she wasn't a sweet old lady, but I didn't argue.

"How about for just a second so I can find a picture of your aunt, we really need it for the obituary and that kind of thing."

"Okay, yeah, sure."

"What's your name?" I asked.

"Kyle Bradbury. Am I going to be in the news?" He looked

equally excited and fearful of that prospect. Which was probably the right reaction.

"Maybe, if that's okay."

"I'm not sure. Like I said, I don't know what to say."

"First off, is there a room where your aunt has pictures or photo albums?"

"Uh, not many but, how about I show you her bedroom, there's stuff in there. I didn't go in there, you know, out of respect."

"Sure, I just want to find a picture. I promise I'll leave everything else alone."

"Uh, okay." Kyle showed me the way. He walked on his tiptoes a bit and shook his left hand at the wrist for no particular reason that I could see.

"You don't have to hang with me if I was interrupting something."

"I'll be in the kitchen then; I was microwaving some mini-pizzas."

"Cool. Let me look in the kitchen really quick. Sometimes people keep pictures on the fridge." I was taking over, that was one of my skill sets. I could get comfortable quickly in someone else's house. As a reporter, I'd been in a hundred homes and had to find a way to connect with the people that lived there fast.

Kyle nodded. He was doing what I said. I knew how to boss around a twenty-something young man if I knew anything.

The house was meticulous. It looked frozen in time. Nothing was out of place except random stuff thrown about by Kyle, I assumed. Not a speck of décor was of this time. It felt like a trip back to the 1940s or earlier. Lottie could have given advice on authentic antique décor. Though from what I'd heard, Lottie wasn't much a giver of anything.

I walked into the kitchen and saw no signs of what had recently happened. I wondered how long Lottie's body would have been in this kitchen if it hadn't been for the UPS guy who found her.

The smell of cleaning products lingered in the space. Kyle didn't look like the kind of guy who would have cleaned up the kitchen, but I didn't know him at all. He lit up a cigarette while I looked around. Cigarettes and bleach were not a great combo.

I wondered if it was smart to have the place cleaned so quickly. Did Loof miss a clue now that the place was scrubbed of what had happened here? Did he release the scene of the crime a little fast? I didn't know the standard operating procedure of the Widow's Bay Police Department and wondered if they even did where murders were concerned.

Other than the bleach smell, there really were no signs of the 21st century at all in this place.

Despite the woman's affinity for collecting errant balls, Lottie was no hoarder, and there wasn't much to even show who lived there.

Lottie's oven and stove were from the 1950s or maybe the 1940s. The name Wedgewood was imprinted on the stove's backsplash.

Her refrigerator was a vintage piece too. It was free of the typical children's drawings or school portraits. Kyle didn't seem to care what I did, so I took a quick peek inside.

To my surprise, it was packed with soup. Row after row of plastic containers of soup.

I wondered who in the world all that soup would be for considering Lottie was such a loner, and Kyle looked more like a Cheetos eater if he ate anything at all.

"Did your aunt make all this soup for you?"

"No, it was just here. I'm going to have to throw it out, I think."

"So how often did you see your aunt?"

"Not a lot, summers. My parents moved us out of Widow's

Bay before I could remember, but they visited Aunt Lottie now and then. They're dead."

"Oh, so you're the only relative?"

"Yep, that's right. Aunt Lottie had a soft spot for me. She loved kids." Kyle Bradbury was lying. Or rather just making things up that he thought sounded suitable for the news.

"And it looked like she loved to cook, soup at least."

"Yeah, sweet, huh?"

"Very. Anything else we should know about your aunt?"

"Uh, no. Just that she was nice, and more like a great great aunt or something. She was super old, like one-hundred."

"Right. I'll just check her bedroom, see if there are any photos of her."

"Sounds good."

I walked out of the kitchen, hoping to find some sort of picture of Lottie to use. Kyle sat down at the kitchen table and continued to drag on his cig. Fine. Stay out of my way if the best quote you've got is, "she was nice."

I walked down the hall to the bedrooms and, finally, on top of a mirrored dresser, was a neat row of framed pictures.

None of the photos looked new. More than half were black and white. I slowly scanned each photo.

One caught my eye. It looked to be the same vintage as Lottie's kitchen appliances, from the clothing, it looked like vintage World War II era.

I zoned in on the face of a pretty woman wearing pants. She looked like a smaller Katherine Hepburn. And she was standing next to a bike. Behind her, a man, broad through the shoulders, had an arm around her waist. The man looked at the woman, and the woman looked right into the camera lens.

It was beautiful, and it was Lottie. Not the Lottie that everyone around here knew but a younger version, a stronger version, and a version of Lottie that seemed to love life. Lottie had never been married. I wondered who the man was. He was rugged looking, handsome, his hair was light, and his gaze was directed to Lottie.

Oh, Lottie, what were you up to during the war?

I took a picture of the picture with my phone. But I'd need something a little more portrait-like though for the paper. I perused all the framed photos that showed Lottie at different stages, mostly with a group of women, and I realized she was with the Distinguished Ladies Club.

I recognized Aunt Dorothy right away, but I think I could also point out Frances Corey, Maxine Proctor, Elsie Faulkner, and Jane Parris. Jane had died a short bit ago, a broken hip or something. I remembered it was in Your U.P. News when I was deciding whether to take the job.

The ladies were all pretty, distinctive, and looked modern even through the decades and with the faded black and white photos.

There was a shot of Aunt Dorothy taking the oath of office as Widow's Bay Mayor in the 1950s. Dorothy wore a tweed suit that skimmed her trim figure. These days Aunt Dorothy was a bit softer. I snapped a photo of the swearing-in. Maybe Candy wasn't such a trailblazer. After all, Aunt Dorothy had been there and done that.

Next to Dorothy at the swearing-in was Lottie. Lottie was smiling. No one had seen Lottie smile in over forty years from what I'd found out, but here was proof that she was physiologically capable of it.

The group shot of the Distinguished Ladies was the best one, I decided. It was bigger than some of the others, it was in color, and Lottie was sitting square with the camera in a formal way, her legs appropriately crossed at the ankle.

It would work for the obits and any other coverage. I studied the photo. What was the occasion? I noted the dresses of the women. They still really matched with who I perceived the older ladies to be today.

Elsie was dressed in a floral print that reminded me of what she wore when she ran a bakery, long since closed, on Main Street. Maxine, the savior of all the town's animals before Fawn, took that mantle, wore a pin with a kitten on her sweater. Jane looked every inch the bombshell, though I didn't know much about her. I also could identify Frances Corey. But there were more than a dozen women in the shot, and I couldn't put a name to all the faces. I did find Lottie easily. She had that same no-frills style in this shot but looked smart. Aunt Dorothy was in the center of the photo, and again with a suit. I wanted to know more about them. About who they were then.

But then I remembered that Dorothy and Elsie at least were driving me insane right now. Maybe it was best to let this obit be quick and smooth instead of risk being alone with Aunt Dorothy any more than I had to right now.

I decided to take the picture out of the frame so I could get a glare-free shot with my camera. I carefully flipped over the frame and moved the hinges to the side. The cardboard matting slid out, and so did a piece of paper.

The paper floated to the ground. I ignored it for a second. I concentrated on positioning the photo on the dresser and was able to get a shot of it free of glare. I also took a picture of the back side of the photo, on which someone had written in neat cursive, Distinguished Ladies, 1949. That would be good for the caption. Ugh, I really needed to make Aunt Dorothy give me a quote. Or maybe I could sidestep her and track down Frances or Maxine. They hadn't said anything bat dung crazy to me, yet.

I replaced the glass and bent down to retrieve the paper that Lottie had stashed behind the photo. The paper was not vintage and might well have been the newest thing in the house.

And I recognized it immediately.

This was a page from the phone directory of The Widow's Bay Loggers Football Parents. There were a lot of familiar names on it, Pauline, Candy, Fawn, Georgie, Mary Jo, and tons more. Each set of parents was listed next to their son on the team.

Why did Lottie have this, and why did she save it? It was two years old.

Lottie sure as heck wasn't a football fan.

And someone had drawn a red line through several names.

Thirteen names, to be exact.

I realized with a shiver, the lines were scratched through the names of the thirteen dads who'd died in the bus crash fundraiser.

I shoved the list and the picture into my bag. I wanted to follow up on the ladies and the list I'd found. Maybe it was nothing, but it felt like something. And it also felt, well, evil.

Kyle Bradbury was clueless as far as I could tell and wouldn't miss it. I'd return it later.

I looked around the room again. I was overwhelmed with the desire to get the heck out of Lottie's house.

"All set, Kyle, I'll show myself out!" I swiftly made my way to the door and out of the bleach and cigarette smoke-choked air.

I took a deep breath as the door closed behind me.

I was totally and completely creeped out.

CHAPTER 9

$\mathcal{I}$ went back to my small office and file my two stories of the day. I also uploaded the convenience store snowmobile crash video, so Your U.P. News readers could get to work on that case.

I started work on the Lottie follow up story. I looked at the photos I was going to send in with the article of a happy looking Lottie Bradbury.

I ran through what I knew about this murder.

Loof said there was no forced entry, she was stabbed in the neck, and there were zero witnesses to anything suspicious happening in her neighborhood. The delivery man, who visited nearly every day, found her dead in the kitchen.

I'd learned today that at some point in the past, Lottie Bradbury was a nice person or at least one who did stuff in the community. She was in love once. And thanks to confirmation from Aunt Dorothy and the nephew Lottie was older than anyone guessed. Despite her old age, it took a stabbing to the neck to kill her.

I was frustrated that no one would give me one warm quote about the woman and her nephew's memories of her were bland at best. The weirdest aspect so far wasn't her age, but the fact that she kept a list of names of the recently departed residents of Widow's Bay.

I decided to make one call before I finished the story. It was my last-ditch attempt to get someone in Lottie's hometown of one-hundred or so years to say one nice thing about her.

The little office for Your U.P. News had a few resources that came in handy when the internet didn't, and one of those was a phone book. Luckily, the women I needed were all listed in the old-fashioned phone book.

In the photos that showed the Distinguished Ladies of Widow's Bay, there were six women consistently in each picture. Lottie was, of course, gone, and Jane was too. That left Maxine, who'd given me the evil eye at the crime scene, Elsie who seemed confused, and my Aunt Dorothy who'd already blown off my questions about Lottie. That left only one more lady that was still alive and in the photos. Frances Corey. Maybe she could say something nice.

Once I talked to her, I'd put the idea of an obituary to bed and just keep up with the investigation. It wasn't my job to do obits, but something compelled me to make this work.

I dialed, and three rings later, an airy voice answered.

"Hello, Marzenna."

"How did you know?"

"That's my thing, knowing."

"Uh, well, neat. I'm calling about Lottie Bradbury."

"Oh?"

"You knew she was murdered?"

"I knew she was gone, yes."

"Can I ask you a few questions about her?"

"Certainly." Finally. Someone to talk to. Sure, she'd just claimed to be quasi-psychic, but at this point, beggars couldn't be choosers.

"What was she like, back in the day, like during the war?"

"Always so strong, pretty, such wit."

"Was she ever in love? Maybe with a ruggedly handsome man?"

"She was, she never forgave Carlisle either."

"For what?"

"For not saving her brother."

"I'm sorry, Carlisle could have saved her brother how?"

"Oh, you know, I'm sure your aunt has explained it. They can offer immortal life, or healing powers, or any number of things, but Lottie's brother... it really wouldn't have helped. Carlisle did the right thing, but Lottie couldn't see it."

Frances was telling me a story from the middle, she assumed I knew it all. I didn't, and here we were again with the mystical. I'd wanted a quote about Lottie Bradbury's volunteer work, and I was down some eternal life and heartbreak path.

"Look, I just need a nice, non-magical quote about the untimely death of an elderly member of our community." I probably shouldn't have been that blunt, but I'd really had enough.

"She was the most powerful, how could you not mention that?"

"Mrs. Corey, just for the obit, the paper, maybe can I say that you said she was strong, pretty, and witty?"

"That is true. That would be fine. And you can say she was instrumental with The Distinguished Ladies Club, well until she started fighting with your Aunt."

"Can you tell me why they fought?"

"That gate, always that gate." Great, the gate. We were one second away from goblins, and I just couldn't.

"Uh, no, forget it. How about this-- I'm going to shift gears. Why, do you think, would Lottie have a list of local football moms and dads? Did she like sports?"

"Oh, the ones who died in that bus crash? Dorothy was right! Terrible, just terrible." Frances' voice changed from confident to amazement. Frances did not, however, seem surprised by my shifting gears. And how did she know what I was refer-ring to?

"What was Aunt Dorothy, right about?"

"Dear, it's all about the gate, getting it open. And now that it is. Well, you better talk to your Aunt soon, or things will be out of control here in Widow's Bay. I've already had two in my shed!"

"Two what?"

"Bear shifters, maybe trolls though, they were after my canning. I'd put up a lot of strawberry jam from the summer."

"Bear shifters? Okay. It was great talking to you, Mrs. Corey, I'll let you go now. You've been a big help with the obituary for Lottie."

"I'm glad. And Marzenna, you have a big role to play. I feel it. Maybe the most important one."

"I'm just a reporter here, so no, but thank you."

"And don't forget to get dog food on the way home, remember you're out."

How in the heck did she know that?

The line went dead.

I stared at the phone. Frances Corey was just as loopy as the rest of the Distinguished Ladies. I was starting to think the sweet little old ladies who ran the town dropped acid at their meetings instead of sipped tea.

I blinked it away. None of this was going to work for a by the numbers article in Your U.P. News. I sorted through the crazy and the mystical and realized this story was again, going to have to be short.

I stuck to the facts and typed up a follow-up piece for the murder of Lottie Bradbury. I added the pictures and sprinkled in the little I knew about her.

I left out her love story, what I'd heard about her brother, and of course, the fact that she had a list of the bus crash victims.

But Frances knew all of that.

And so did my Aunt.

I knew I'd have to sit down and hash this out with her. The weird things she was saying, the weird stuff going on in town, I wanted it all to go away. I'd come here for solace, a respite from the dumpster fire marriage and career, a fresh start with my empty nest. Instead, I'd stepped into a town that believed bear shifters were pilfering the canned strawberry jam.

Maybe my Aunt and her friends had concocted a fairy tale they liked to share with each other? Did they collectively settle on some strange mythology and somehow all believe it?

The alternative had bear shifters and trolls robbing from old ladies in broad daylight and tragic WWII era vampire love stories.

It was time to call it a day. I did a final check of my email. Justin sent me a reminder to follow up on the logging story tomorrow.

I shot off an email and agreed to check it out. A day off from murders and psychics sounded like exactly what I needed.

Tomorrow I'd focus on tedious economic development, public-private partnerships, and regulations! If I were lucky, we'd get into zoning ordinances.

Nothing said mundane, like a story about government permits. I needed a little mundane.

Oh, and dog food.

CHAPTER 10

I'd gone from feeding my husband, the boys, and their friends in a frenzy after work, to feeding Bubba and Agnes.

And apparently, everyone on the Psychic Hotline knew Bubba was out of food.

Luckily, it was going to be easier to get his special, favorite, fancy dog food now that I was back home in Widow's Bay.

I ordered it online from none other than Fawn. She had a profitable side business selling organic pet food.

Now I could just go get it and haul it home.

Fawn's clinic was at the edge of downtown Widow's Bay. It was where the thriving metropolis, as they jokingly referred to the three-traffic light downtown, petered out into the vast open space of the rest of their county. Fawn was able to live and work there. Her location made it easy for pet owners to get to from downtown, and easy for her to live with her menagerie of animals of the great white north. Fawn housed animals of all sorts that needed her help or needed a home.

Fawn was always a few steps from the wild, especially back when we were kids. She'd grown into a responsible scientist, mom, and business owner. But her wild streak was there, just under the surface. That was a strong pull of Widow's Bay, my friends. We knew each other's history, dreams, tragedies, and victories. I loved Fawn, Georgie, and Tatum. They were the sisters I never had. I feared I'd roamed too far from this town in my life to understand what was happening here now.

As strange as the last few days here at been, it warmed me down to my bones to live close to Fawn, Tatum, and Georgie. I'd lost a family, and they were here to remind me that I wasn't alone.

Fawn's family all worked at Bay Mills Casino, the first Indian owned Casino in Michigan. Her dad wanted her to follow in his footsteps into the business. But caring for animals was always Fawn's passion, and plan, not poker tables.

When I got to the clinic, her waiting room was full. Fawn always took patients during odd hours. She knew people couldn't take off work for their own health care, much less for their animals, so Fawn was there early or late, at lunch, and on weekends to keep the furry denizens of Widow's Bay healthy.

Her receptionist was young. Her nametag read Savanah.

"Hi, I'm Fawn's friend Marzie. Looks pretty busy here right now."

"It's been nuts today, tons of pets acting up." Savanah was a pretty blonde who couldn't be too far out of high school. I had to give anyone who worked in the vet clinic credit. It meant handling an incredible amount of fur, poop, and dog drool.

"Can you ring me up the big bag of Fawn's Big Paw Organic?" Bubba Smith loved Fawn's Big Paw Dog Food more than almost anything in the world, excluding Agnes.

"That's a thirty-pound bag. If you unlock your vehicle, I can have Tyler our vet assistant load it for you."

"Thank you."

"And I'm sure Dr. Campana would love you to pop in and say hi. Exam room four."

I walked back to the exam room, and there was Fawn, patiently listening to a worried pet owner.

"I found my Precious Moments, my limited issued Green Bay Packers one, in the toilet. She's done it three times, haven't you Breathless?" I waited outside the door as Fawn dealt with the pet issue at hand.

"Last month, it was what?" Fawn asked the incredibly frustrated owner of a cat named Breathless.

"Last month she tried to flush Humphrey the Camel and Inky down the toilet. Those two Beanies are worth hundreds! I used the blow dryer on them, but it has to affect value, a dunk in the toilet, don't you think?"

Fawn gave her best advice and answer.

"Well, that's more a question for the Antiques Roadshow. The one thing you have to know about Breathless Mahoney is she's smart. She knows those Beanies and collectibles are worth a lot to you. Maybe she's jealous? You've got a couple of choices. You can either lock up your collectibles. Get a curio with a key type of thing. Or lock the toilet seat. With one of those baby proof latches."

"Can't I just train her not to do it?" The worried owner asked Fawn. I peeked around the corner to see Breathless Mahoney giving herself a bath while the concerned humans talked.

"In my experience, no. Cats do what they want, without exception." Fawn said and scratched behind the ears of the dastardly Breathless Mahoney. I swear that cat rolled her eyes.

"Hundreds, I mean HUNDREDS of dollars. I don't think those Beanies are going to ever be the same." Breathless Mahoney's human was an older lady, not quite Distinguished Ladies level of elderly, but maybe in her sixties. Her hair was teased, sprayed, and a bright shade of red. She also appeared as worried as a person could be about a misbehaving cat. I had one, so I could relate.

I moved aside as she walked out of the exam room with the

REBECCA REGNIER

collectible murdering cat in the crook of her arm. From my vantage point, Fawn had given Breathless and her owner a viable plan of action.

Fawn walked over to her sink, washed her hands, and shook her head. Her massive amount of dark hair bobbled a little; she had it loosely piled up on top of her head. If the world could trace the origin of the messy bun, it would lead directly to Fawn.

"There's no way in hell those Beanies are worth money, right?" She asked me as she dried her hands off.

"Well, certainly not now that they've had a swirly courtesy of Breathless Mahoney." We both laughed, and I hugged my friend. Where Tatum was tough, intense, and a shrewd business owner, Fawn was as nurturing to humans as she was to pets. It was easy to take advantage of her giving nature. I made a mental note to find a way to fill her bucket instead of always dip from it.

"I just swung by to get some feed for Bubba, looks like you're busy as heck."

"Crazy busy, almost everyone in town has a behavior issue with their pets today, down to a hamster who wouldn't get off his wheel. Poor little thing was in full sprint with his tiny legs for over fifteen hours."

"What was the prescription?"

"Take the wheel out of the cage."

"Sometimes, the obvious solution is the right one, eh?"

"Yeah, eight years of school for that medical prognosis."

Sometimes I worried that Fawn, of all my friends, she was still in the most profound grief after her husband died in the Casino Bus trip fundraiser. Fawn was the least like herself. She tended to blame herself. Her family worked at the casino, so she felt at fault.

To cope, Fawn, like the rest of the now single ladies of Widow's Bay, immersed herself in her work. Tatum's bar, Georgie's bookstore, even Pauline's real estate, and fitness classes. All of those things blossomed in the last few years. I took note. It was a comfort to find joy in your profession when your kids didn't need you to make peanut butter and jelly anymore.

But today, there was a light in Fawn's eyes. The purpose she had, taking care of animals, was maybe outweighing the loss she experienced, and the unearned guilt over that trip. I hoped so.

"Anything new with the murder of Lottie Bradbury?" Fawn asked.

"A few things, I mean no leads or clues, or suspects but I talked to her nephew and her friend, Frances Corey, another of the nutball Distinguished Ladies, and at least I can get some sort of follow up together."

"On that, I think I've got her cat."

"Really? I remember Maxine muttering something about that when we were out there at the crime scene."

"Yeah, a Siamese. Lottie brought her in here before, and a neighbor dropped her in last night. Wandering, clearly an indoor cat. Her name is Theodora. I'll maybe see if Maxine wants to take care of her. God knows I don't have room right now."

"Fawn, it's getting weirder and weirder. Did I forget how extra Widow's Bay was while I was away, or is something happening?"

"I think both."

"We're getting together tomorrow night, right. We can compare notes on what's happening around here?" Fawn didn't seem worried about it or slightly panicked like I felt.

"Mrs. Corey said something about bear shifters getting into her canning, and my Aunt, I mean Vampires?

"Well, yeah, I know. Some people see some people don't, and there's you."

"What do you mean?"

"You see, but you don't believe."

"Maybe."

"If we have something extra, or magic, is it all that farfetched? You can't have completely forgotten what we could do as kids?"

"You're a scientist, how can you even let this crazy talk not freak you out?"

"Nature, science, and even forces we can't explain are connected. Maybe it's all nature that we haven't scienced up yet."

"I wish I was as centered as you. What's your secret?"

"Maybe it's that I spend more time with animals than I do with the Distinguished Ladies." She smiled, and it helped me calm down. As crazy as the first few days in Widow's Bay was, Fawn wasn't nuts. She could accept the weird and the mundane in one package. I needed to take a page out of her book.

"Thanks, Fawn. I'll let you go. Bubba Smith is probably hungry for dinner."

Tyler popped his head in.

"Food's in your Jeep, and Doc, the waiting room is stacking up. Savannah said to tell you."

"I'm out of here. See you tomorrow night." I left my pretty friend to her patients.

I walked through the exam area and toward the waiting room.

I nearly tripped over a furry little white ball of fluff, and without hesitation, I crouched down to pick it up.

It was the most beautiful little puppy. It looked part Siberian Husky or Samoyed maybe? It was snowy white.

I stood up and pet the little guy. He nuzzled in and seemed perfectly happy to be snuggled by a stranger.

"Who do you belong to little boy?" I asked and figured I'd deposit the fluff ball with Savannah. I couldn't help scratch behind his fluffy ears.

"Ah, there you are!" At the entrance to the waiting room was the guy from the spinning class.

"You missing this little tyke?"

"Yes, doesn't know when to stay put." He was just as good looking as I'd remembered. His auburn hair was loose, and he was clearly one of the new loggers. If his lumberjack flannel was a clue or a costume, he sure looked the part anyway.

I tried to give the cute puppy back, and he licked my face.

"He likes you."

"Yeah, I like him too." I carefully moved the warm bundle into his owner's arms.

"Thanks for intercepting. His little legs move faster than you'd expect."

"No problem." I left the handsome puppy owner to melt Savannah or Fawn's heart. What a combo that guy was.

I turned and walked out through the waiting room and noticed it was busy like Fawn had said. There were neighbors with all manner of pets on leashes, in cages, and on laps.

And there were also a couple of faces that didn't look anything like the Widow's Bay residents I knew.

There were a lot of male faces, handsome ones, rugged ones, waiting on Fawn.

Were they all here for the logging jobs that Candy mentioned? Were people showing up in advance of the All Souls Festival? Did they work at the Samhain Slopes? My small town was getting bigger every day.

I realized I had a million threads to pull, stories to dig into, but above all, I had a hungry dog at home to feed.

Like Fawn said, hanging out with furry friends might be the key to my mental health.

Of course, that excluded Agnes, who was driving me to crazy town faster than my Aunt.

I walked out to the Jeep and pointed it toward my new home.

Unpacking, a glass of wine, and rest. That's what I needed after a day that saw the universe tilt on a bizarre angle.

CHAPTER 11

*B*y the time I got home, the sun was down.

I pulled in and opened the hatch of my Jeep Wrangler to retrieve the food for my housemates. There was a certain freedom in not having to rush home in accordance with other people's work or school schedule. I'd discovered I liked it.

When the boys were little guilt hovered around me, not so much when I was at work -- I never felt guilty about work. But guilt crept in when I went shopping or commuted or did anything other than work or mom stuff. Shaking off the pressure that I was taking away from someone else by doing something for me was slow, and surprisingly worth it.

And my animals were happiest when I was benignly ignoring them, so I didn't have to rush home from anywhere.

Unfortunately, a thirty-pound bag was a bit heavier than I thought, and I needed to haul that sucker myself.

I balanced it on one shoulder and struggled to walk to my door.

This was the annoying part about singlehood. There was no one but me to bring stuff in from the car. That was a thing you took for granted with sons and a husband, there were schlep helpers.

Where's the Pinterest Board for that? *Till Schlep Do Us Part,* written on a chalkboard in lovely calligraphy when you got married. That would be more accurate than the actual vows. *I promise to love, honor, and carry your crap into the car or out to the curb.*

I got the bag lifted, barely, and headed to the back door. I tried to hang on to the awkward weight of the bag and unlock the back door, but I couldn't quite manage the task. I lost the battle against the dog food, and I lost my grip on it. It dropped to my feet and took me out!

I hurled backward off my porch step. In that split second, I braced for my tailbone to hit the concrete.

Instead, something broke my fall, and I landed softly without the expected crunch.

In fact, I didn't hit the ground at all. Mercifully.

A firm hand had bolstered me from behind.

"Whoa? Thank you." I said to whoever had been at the right place at the right time to prevent me from breaking a hip like poor departed Jane Parris.

I scrambled to find my footing and turn around.

I had to blink to be sure I was seeing who I was seeing.

It was the white-haired, fur-wearing, blue-eyed, Viking-style, dream dude from hallucination land. And he was real.

And he was named Stephen Brule. I couldn't deny that I had seen him at the ski lodge, the Frog Toe, and in my weird dream. He was everywhere. This time he was no figment. I'd biffed it, and he'd saved me from breaking my backside.

"You're welcome."

I found myself staring. Brule was tall, broad at the shoulders, and really did have the bluest eyes I'd ever seen. His hair was white, he had very fine lines around the temples and a few deeper ones around his mouth. He had almost a cartoonishly strong jaw, narrow lips, and snow-white teeth.

I realized I was a little overwhelmed by the rugged handsomeness of Stephen Brule and his hint of a French accent. Maybe that's why I'd dreamed about him? He stood out.

I was also more than a little concerned that a massive hot flash was working its way from my chest to my hairline at this inopportune moment. I also wondered if I smelled like the vet clinic, bleach, or cigarette smoke. All were a possibility considering my day.

I shook it off. The man was not here to pick me up for a date. He was here to pick me up from nearly breaking my hip like an octogenarian.

"Let me carry this package into your home."

"Oh, could you? I overestimated my ability to haul this thing."

"You should not have to."

"Yeah, where are those servants when you need them?" I quipped, mainly because when I was nervous, sarcasm reared its ugly head.

"Let me open the door." I unlocked the door and stepped in and held it open for Stephen Brule.

"I may enter?"

"You may." I smiled at the very dignified way he posed the question. I mean, I had my arm extended and directing him in, but still, he asked.

Mr. Brule effortlessly hoisted the bag up and followed me into the mudroom.

"Just put it right there. I keep all the dog stuff in here." He put the bag down and as if on cue Bubba Smith walked into the kitchen and looked at us both. Agnes, of course, was on his back. She regarded Brule for only a second and was able to pass her judgment.

Handsome. Too bad you're wearing that frumpy coat.

I narrowed my eyes at my cat and at Bubba Smith. Bubba turned and walked them both into another room.

"I have never seen a cat use a dog for transportation in that fashion."

"Yeah, she thinks she's Miss Daisy."

"Miss Daisy?"

"You know, as in Driving Miss Daisy."

"No, I do not know."

I was just about to start babbling. I could feel it coming on like a sneeze, and this man's blue eyes had to be the reason. I wasn't a woman who got rattled in front of men, but Mr. Brule was different.

He'd appeared out of nowhere in the middle of the bar fight, and boom he was here at my house when I'd not told him where I lived.

That realization had me questioning whether I should have let him in at all.

Instead of telling him thanks and get out like I should have, word salad started shooting out of my mouth.

"Morgan Freeman, Jessica Tandy, and he's the chauffeur? And Dan Aykroyd with a surprise appearance in a dramatic movie."

"Oh, it is a movie."

"Yeah, kind of a famous one. Okay, forget it. Can I get you something to drink?"

"Merci." We made our way into my kitchen. I busied myself hanging up my coat and finding glasses. I had transported zero housewares in my move. Aunt Dorothy said the kitchen here was stocked, I just didn't know where the heck anything was yet.

"This kitchen hasn't changed."

"Excuse me?" Mr. Brule was looking around the room. "I used to own this house, many of the houses around here."

As far as I knew, my family had owned this house for decades. "I think you're probably mistaking this one for another one. We've had this for years, grew up here actually."

"You left Widow's Bay after your schooling?"

"To continue my schooling, as you put it. I went away to college, and it stuck. But thanks to a friggin' asshole ex-husband and YouTube, I'm back."

"I have heard of this YouTube."

"Good. Yeah, I lost my cool on television, and as a news anchor, that's frowned upon."

"And the husband, did he hurt you?" Brule looked concerned, protective almost.

"Only my pride, shacked up with a younger woman. Classic mid-life crisis."

"It is an old story. I can never understand it."

"What?"

"I cannot understand voluntarily spending time with younger women. A woman with some patina, that's more interesting." I filled the water glasses I'd found to brush off the comment directed at my patina.

"Right. Patina." That sounded better than wrinkles anyway. This guy was good, very good. Shoot. I needed to order a satin pillow, so I didn't make the patina worse. I snapped out of my ADD, and I pulled out a chair and indicated that we should sit down. It made me more comfortable sitting instead of standing awkwardly in my kitchen.

I handed him a glass of water.

"Sorry, I'd offer you something else, wine, pop, but I haven't really unpacked or stocked up. Except for the behemoth amount of dog food that nearly killed me."

"Water is fine. I will have some wine sent to you."

"Uh, what?"

"The wines at Samhain Slopes are excellent."

"Cool, no need, but thank you. So how did you find this place, decide to invest here?" I decided that the best bet would be to put on my reporter hat. The big deal investor, for the most significant thing going in Widow's Bay, heck the county, was in my kitchen.

"I love this land; this soil is my true earth. I knew the gate would be opened one way or another. Though I couldn't return I, have watched Widow's Bay from afar all these years. It needed us as much as we needed it."

The gate again. Where Aunt Dorothy and her old friends were clearly one foot in loony town, Brule was a business owner, an entrepreneur, and investor. Maybe he could make some sane sense of this whole thing. I took a deep breath and dove in.

"What is the gate? What do you mean?"

"I have promised your Aunt Dorothy and the others not to reveal too much."

"What... look, they're nuts. You seem marginally sane. Whatever they're talking about, I'd steer clear if I were you. Their meds are off, you know what I mean? Something clogged somewhere." I pointed to the back of my neck.

"No. I do not know what you mean. You talk fast and make little sense." I tried not to turn red at that characterization.

"Well then work a little harder to keep up. Whatever my Aunt is talking about lately is cuckoo for Cocoa Puffs."

"Dorothy is as sane as you are. From the looks of things probably saner. I do not know how she put up with that awful woman for as long as she did. Your Aunt has always honored the vow. Some of us were barely alive, hunted into hiding. But your Aunt found a way for us again, finally."

Brule smiled and sipped his water.

"What awful women? Lottie? Honestly, why are you here?"

"I told you, this is our ancestral home. Mine and the others. We need to be here for our safety and our lives."

"Stop talking like that. You're supposed to say economic development, okay? And I meant, why are you in my kitchen?"

"You invited me. Keep that in mind, by the way." His stare was unnerving. I needed to figure out what was what. I stood up and walked to the sink with our water glasses.

"You're talking in circles. I'm about five minutes from packing up my cat and dog and getting out of Dodge. I mean, I'd miss my friends, but I've done it before."

I turned around, and there he was, standing in front of me. We were less than an inch apart.

I'd be lying if I said I wasn't attracted to him. He was the most handsome man I'd ever seen, he was mysterious, and for some reason, he kept seeking me out.

"Marzenna, fear not. You have a role to play though you do not know it. That is the fault of your elders. Not you."

"My elders?"

"We are powerfully connected you and me. Your role is vital to Widow's Bay."

"I'm a reporter for a rinky-dink online newspaper, ex-wife, and mother to adult sons. That's what I'm connected to."

"You're more than that. You've just begun to discover all you are meant for."

My breath was caught in my throat. Brule reached out and touched my cheek. I didn't know what to say or do. My experience in flirting with charismatic rich Europeans was exactly zero. I felt an urge to put my hand on his chest. And there was a connection between us. I recognized him. I reacted to him.

And I didn't know the first thing about him.

So, I completely chickened out. I had already decided today was too much, weird, over the top, and now here I was with a man about to kiss me?

"I think you should go. Thank you for the help with the kibble."

"I've waited decades for right now. I can wait a few more days."

I closed my eyes to center myself, to process, and when I opened them back up again, he was gone. Completely gone.

I walked over to the door and looked outside. There was no Brule or even a car he might have driving in. As quickly as he appeared, he disappeared.

I looked up and down my street. Where had he gone? Nothing looked out of place.

But something sounded out of place.

There was howling in the distance.

But from the sound of it. Not distant enough for comfort.

CHAPTER 12

*I*n a shocking turn of events, I had a fitful night of sleep and odd as heck dreams.

Handsome Frenchmen wanting to kiss me? Check.

Howling animals? Check.

Talking cats? Yep.

Murderer on the loose? Check.

Oh, wait. That was my real life.

I smoothed out the pillowcase marks on my face and remembered that I was supposed to sleep on a satin pillow or similar, so my right cheek didn't look like a stretch of bad road during a drought when I got up in the morning.

Today I was skipping the workout. Sorry, Pauline. I checked the email on my phone, ordered my face-saving pillowcase, and sent an email to Justin all before the sun rose.

Candy, let me know where the offices were for the new logging operations. I was going to see what I could see. If there was activity, I'd have a story.

I knew for sure there were dozens of new faces in Widow's Bay. A lot of them needed a shave and looked like the descendants of Paul Bunyan. That had to mean the logging operations were swinging. Even if they didn't yet have an all-clear from all the different zoning dictators up and down the state.

I'd done a little homework on this. Thanks to Georgie's local history treasure trove at The Broken Spine, I knew something about logging, mining, and the history of the U.P.'s economy.

Everywhere else in Michigan economies, and the rise and fall of towns, were stories about automotive companies, here though, it was what was on the land or in it that made Widow's Bay.

Before the 1900s, logging was the primary industry for Widow's Bay until all the trees were gone. And the loggers moved west.

Now, though, thanks to forest management, the forests of the U.P. were healthy, lush, dense even, and ready for a new era of responsible harvesting of the natural resources. They called it Sustainable Forestry these days.

Whatever the name, it looked like new jobs could be on the way if Candy got her way instead of Ridge. Candy was full speed on tourism for the short term and logging for the long haul.

Ridge was happy to "not in my backyard" every plan that was in front of the Widow's Bay City Council. He wanted copper mining or nothing at all.

Candy said the new logging owners were going to retool and hoped to reopen a sawmill that was over one-hundred-fifty years old. North Woods Lumber Company had been abandoned longer than I'd, or even my parents had been alive.

Like a lot of things in this part of the country, there wasn't a GPS guide to get you where you were going, I hoped my memory of the area served me.

The sun was losing in a battle with the overcast clouds so far today. It was after sunrise, but you wouldn't really know it. That and the tall white pines muted whatever daylight wanted to rise on the outskirts of Widow's Bay. I drove slowly with my headlights on along the winding old county roads.

I was ten miles outside of Widow's Bay proper, but it felt like I was a million miles from any other person. I hadn't quite gotten used to the solitude that being here again meant. At any given stretch of any given trip, you could feel utterly alone and isolated on the road.

I knew what I was looking for, though. The entrance to the mill was tough to spot, but I found it. The sign was still there. Whoever planted it in the often-frozen ground, over 150 years ago, sunk it deep.

I directed my headlights to the sign, North Woods Lumber Company, established 1860. I rolled slowly up the drive and toward the main building.

If the business was opening, it sure wasn't going to be today. I was pretty sure this was going to be a wasted trip. I zipped my coat up to my chin and decided to grab my fancy camera instead of my cell phone. Let Justin see some beautiful shots of nature, if not an actual interview.

There was a massive warehouse-style building. That had to be where they stored equipment or lumber. I looked around and found a smaller outbuilding that I pegged as the offices. It was as good a place as any to start. I walked across the compound.

Maybe the manager or owner was around to answer some questions. That would be enough for a story. The door wasn't boarded up like on the main building. Maybe someone was here.

I gave a loud knock on the door.

"Hello! I'm from the Your U.P. News! I'm looking for the owner or manager?"

I banged on the door again. I peeked in the office window. But it was dark, and I couldn't see much.

I decided to look around and see if there were any other signs of life at the mill.

I walked around to the back of the larger building, just to check things out and see if any work had begun. I didn't find any employees, but I did hit the jackpot.

There were two rows of heavy equipment. Giant rigs parked

neatly next to one another. I had no idea what they were called, but it was clear the equipment was there for breaking down and hauling timber. They were bright yellow and looked unused so far, but they sure as heck weren't vintage 1860.

I took a few photos. Even if I didn't get an interview today, I had proof that something was happening out here. I stepped back from the big rigs and looked around again.

Just beyond the equipment was a path, carved into the dense forest with the giant tires of the rigs I'd seen.

Something was already going on, and I'd get the first story! I did a little internal happy dance on that.

I walked further into the woods on the fresh path.

That's when a howling noise stopped me cold.

Everyone in Widow's Bay knew the sound of coyote, bear, or even wolf. This was a wolf howl for sure.

I'd seen the wolves cross the road the other day, and I knew it wasn't a cause for panic. I may be a city girl now, but I was raised in Widow's Bay.

I did need to keep my head, though. All thoughts about a scoop on the logging operations flew out of it. It was easy to focus on the here and now when you were scared that what you could hear could get here, now.

The howl was full-throated, like the howl I'd heard the other night at my house. And there was more than one voice.

I cursed myself a bit for walking around out here like it was civilized.

The howling got louder, and I ran through the best options for getting back to my Jeep in one piece.

The howling stopped.

That had to be good. I hoped it was anyway. Except now, I couldn't gauge a distance between me and whatever was going on out here.

I took a slow step backward.

Then I saw it. A flash of fur, gray, white, red, black. They streaked across the dirt track in front of me.

I hadn't stumbled upon a wolf. I'd stumbled onto a pack of wolves.

Then the howling started again. One voice, two, three, more? Dozens? I couldn't tell. I heard keening, wailing. I'd bet a million bucks those wolves were crying.

And something moved me forward, not backward. The central trait that led me to become a reporter was curiosity. No matter what weird thing, scary thing, sad thing, or funny thing happened, I wanted to know more. I tried to get closer. Find the source. I put the blame on a lifetime of following that reporter instinct for why I went forward and not back.

I had to see, could I get a shot of it? I imagined the web traffic that photos of a pack of howling wolves could generate. What if there was a new strain of wolves? We could do follow-ups with the DNR. My mind raced.

My new bosses at Your U.P. News would be thrilled.

I walked forward a few more feet. Trying not to rustle anything under my boots, but the howling drowned out whatever sounds I might make as I crept forward.

That's when I saw them. They were gigantic, glorious, really, and terrifying.

A giant grey wolf, a red one behind him, then four more, of black, gray, and brown. They walked in a straight line. There was even a puppy! These were no ordinary Michigan gray wolves. These were hybrids of some kind. They had to be.

They also didn't look like each other. Each had its own markings, its own body shape. Instead of a litter, they looked to be a mishmash of different wolf breeds. Or better yet the breed standards for the Wolfminster Dog Show. Their coats were shiny and lush, not matted, or mangy like you'd expect of a wild animal.

They stopped howling, and the straight line they'd walked in curved into itself and formed a circle. I dropped down as low as I could behind some brush.

The red wolf began to dig furiously. The wolves sat at attention as he did. Then he stopped, and the gray wolf dropped something from his mouth into the circle. They were burying something. A black wolf kicked dirt over whatever they'd buried.

The circle of wolves began to rotate, and the big grey lifted his snout in the air and let out a howl so piercing that I had to cover my ears. Then the red, the black, the smaller grey, the red, all of them howled together.

It almost looked like a ceremony or a funeral. If wild animals had official events, I was spying on one.

The wolves were focused on their ritual or whatever it was. But at any moment they could decide I was more interesting. The best-case scenario was that I was an intruder, the worst-case scenario, I was prey.

I sat still, handled my breathing as best as I could manage, and hoped I could wait them out.

I couldn't really tell if the gray wolf or the red wolf was in charge. Was there an alpha wolf? Was that how it worked? Fawn would know. I mentally begged for Fawn to give me guidance. Praying to my vet friend, as a strategy, probably wasn't a good one. I wished like hell that she was here, and for a moment, I reached out to her for help with my mind. What would she do? How would she behave if she were in my place? Fawn, you won't believe what I'm seeing!

There was no doubt, though, who the omega was: the puppy. The other wolves nipped at him if he got distracted by a sound or an interesting leaf and herded him back into their circle. The puppy looked familiar to me, but I didn't have the luxury of thinking about anything but survival.

Then as if by mutual agreement, the wolf dance abruptly stopped. They stayed in a circle, but they were still. The gray lifted his face to the sky and howled. The six I could see chimed in. My eyes watered from it, the tone, the volume, the pain. I heard keening all around me. Not just from the wolves in the circle. It dawned on me that other howls and noises were vibrating behind me.

I wasn't safe, or protected, or hidden. There were wolves all over the place, not just in this circle. I was in mortal danger. And yet I'd never seen anything so magical in my life. I knew I wasn't supposed to see this, but there I was.

I had to take a picture. I had to. Part of me was unsure if this was even happening. I needed a shot. And if I were mauled maybe someone would know why when they found my camera.

I clicked the shutter. And of course, I did it at the exact wrong moment.

The gray stopped. He lowered his head, and then he saw me. They all took cues from him. The howling stopped. The focus shifted, and I was now the center of it.

Howls turned to growls. Each wolf began to growl and bare their teeth. In contrast to the haze of the dull morning, their fangs gleamed.

There was no fighting or even running. This would be it for me. If they decided to rip me to shreds, shredded I would be. They waited.

My instinct was to just stand my ground. At least the last thing I would see would be a magnificent animal as it ripped my head off.

I was backed up against a tree. I had no hope of running back to my Jeep at this point. As they tightened a new circle around me, it appeared there was yet no decision on who would take the first chunk. A streak of fur darted between the others, almost pranced.

And that furball landed at my feet. Now that he was close, I realized where I'd seen him before. At the vet! It was the same little guy from Fawn's vet clinic.

He nudged my leg, whimpered, and I knew he wanted me to pick him up.

If I did it, would they be angry? Would they perceive it as a threat? I didn't have time to analyze anymore. I had no other plan.

I snatched up the puppy while never taking my eyes off the teeth of the other half dozen wolves. It might be my only chance, holding the pup, my new best friend, my volunteer hostage.

It was a desperate plan, and I'd likely be dead, but I'd be dead either way. At least I was trying something, nuts as it was.

The growling intensified, and they closed in. I kissed the pup on the top of the head. I couldn't let the puppy get ripped up with me. I was so screwed.

"Thank you, sweet puppy, good try. Now you better go make friends. You don't want to be in the way of all those teeth coming at me." I put him down. He stupidly hung around my feet. He was going to be collateral damage if this turned into a feeding frenzy. His sweet attempt to protect me made me want to cry.

"None of you are as brave as this little one!" I yelled at the pack.

If I was going to die, I was going to die fighting and facing forward.

I decided to act like the boss I was. I raised two sons, I was a badass reporter, I faced divorce and moved on. They weren't getting a pushover for dinner.

I essentially did to the wolves what I did to my sons when I wanted to get them in line as kids. I stepped forward instead of back, and it confused the hell out of the pack for a second.

"Yes, I am a crazy bitch!" I yelled at them. Every dog had to respect that for a moment, at least.

But it didn't last. Something behind me smashed into my shoulder, and I was down. I was face first in the dirt.

The puppy whined, and then I couldn't see. I was crushed under a massive weight. I heard barks, growls, a few whimpers.

But no bites. I realized I was underneath the red wolf. I contorted myself into a ball.

Amazingly the red had decided the puppy was right and had either planned to protect me or keep me for himself. Whatever his thought process, I couldn't imagine. But he seemed to be ordering the pack to back down.

He was the alpha wolf, that mystery was solved. He ran them off with growls and barks. I stayed small as possible as they scattered off into the trees away from me.

The red had to be close to 200 pounds. He stood at the haunches at least chest-high to me. He was a massive animal, certainly bigger than even my loveable Bubba Smith. I was still on the ground, sitting, leaning back on my hands, and just looking for a cue what to do next.

The red was thick through the chest. I supposed it was easy to tell he was the alpha; I just had no experience in this department at all. I looked into his amber eyes and still didn't move. Then the animal nudged me with his nose. The nudge was enough to practically roll me over, but I took it to mean he wanted me to stand. I tried to stand but stumbled. My head was light; adrenaline was forcing my heart to pump too fast. He came up next to me. Making sure I didn't fall. Miraculously he stood next to me for a moment.

Then I knew. I knew who he was. I knew I'd seen him before.

Or rather I'd seen those amber eyes.

And my perception of what existed in the world cataclysmically shifted forever. I reached out my hand and put it on the red's head.

"You're Grady."

The wolf nodded.

And then he looked behind me.

Someone or something was coming toward us. And they walked on two feet, not four. Thank God.

"Hello! Marzie! We're here!"

Fawn and Aunt Dorothy walked toward me. Aunt Dorothy held on to Fawn's arm for balance on the uneven path. With her other arm, she waved.

The red wolf, Grady, stayed still as they approached.

"How did you find me?"

"I heard you," Fawn said. I thought back. I'd reached out to Fawn in my thoughts when I was trying to figure out how not to die. She'd heard my cry for help somehow.

"I helped her narrow in on where to look for you and such," Aunt Dorothy filled in the gap about why she was here too.

"Oh, Grady, how touching, for Jane?" My Aunt was talking to the wolf. Of course she was.

I turned to look at the red wolf, and somehow the air around him shifted and shimmered. Fawn and I grabbed each other by the arm as the red wolf turned into the man we'd seen at Pauline's class. I knew it was Grady but didn't really know. Until I did. I felt like I might throw up.

Grady, the man, now stood before us. He'd shifted? Was that the word?

Fawn was staring at him like he was a lab experiment, and she held my arm so tight it was the only way I could be sure I wasn't having a hormonally induced nightmare.

I was awake. And I was an inhale and exhale away from hyperventilating.

Aunt Dorothy walked in front of Fawn and me. Her breathing seemed normal. She seemed normal and calm. And I had no idea how that was possible. Aunty Dorothy hugged Grady.

"It's been such a long time. You've grown." She smiled at the wolfman.

"We scared your niece. I'm sorry about that. We were doing the ceremony for Jane and Lottie."

"Lottie too, well, you've got a bigger heart than I do. Thank you. I'll handle it from here. They're not up to speed."

"I can see that."

"And we can all see, well, everything. Grady, best, go find your drawers!" Aunt Dorothy acted like the handsome monster in front of them was a first-grader.

"Aunt Dorothy, I nearly got ripped to pieces by this, ugh, man?" I didn't really know how to put what had just happened into words.

"You don't just walk into a pack ceremony. That's just rude. That's something you need to know. We're so behind with your generation. I blame myself, oh, and social media."

Grady had disappeared into the thick woods, and I looked from Aunt Dorothy to Fawn in hopes of finding something I could hold onto that wasn't impossible.

"Calm down, honey, you're perfectly safe now."

"Right, safe. That's what they told Little Red Riding Hood, I'm guessing."

"Grady was just taking a sniff! It's a compliment."

"Fawn, say something, please."

"I wonder if I can get a sample of his hair or fur?" Fawn was taking this ridiculous situation and trying to put it in a category that made sense for her, science.

"They're quite the specimens, aren't they?" Aunt Dorothy was throwing down serious double entendre.

"We just saw a wolf turn into a… a…. a man?"

"Like the legends of the ancestors." Fawn seemed to be handling this better than I was.

"How right you are," Aunt Dorothy said. They were both handling this better than I was.

I turned and walked back up the path. I wanted out of the woods. I wanted something familiar. I wanted a drink. Was it five yet?

"Slow down! I can't walk that fast anymore." Aunt Dorothy called after me. I did not slow down.

I got to my Jeep and realized that I was completely out of breath. I leaned on it a moment and tried to pull myself together.

What had I just seen? A flipping werewolf?

A few minutes later, Aunt Dorothy and Fawn emerged.

"Can you take your aunt? I have to get right back to patients."

"We need to talk," I said to Fawn.

"Yeah, we do."

"Tonight," I hit the unlock on my car.

"Okay."

"And thank you for saving me." Somehow Fawn had heard my fear, telegraphed across the miles. And she'd acted fast to help me. For that, I was grateful. The bond between my friends and me was stronger than I had guessed.

Grateful was fighting with terrified for space in my head after what had just happened.

I was in awe, angry at Aunt Dorothy, and questioning my own sanity.

Fawn handed Aunt Dorothy off to me.

"Get in," I said and came around to the driver's side.

"You don't have to be snippy." I ignored that.

"I think it's past time you explained what is going on." I started the engine, and we headed back to Widow's Bay.

I needed some answers from Aunt Dorothy, and this time had to admit to myself that something more than old age was happening to her and this town.

"I've been trying to tell you all along," she said and popped down the visor. She fished around in her purse and applied a fresh coat of lipstick.

I shook my head and put my eyes back on the road.

CHAPTER 13

"*I* am jealous, I know the pack ceremonies are just beautiful." Aunt Dorothy said as I tried to return to normal respiration and heart function.

"What?"

"A funeral ceremony for Jane and Lottie. I mean, after all, Lottie did. It's incredible. I mean Jane was their Liaison, but Lottie was just a bitch." Aunt Dorothy continued to act like what I'd just seen was normal.

"Aunt Dorothy, we just saw a wolf turn into a man. I just narrowly escaped becoming a dog biscuit!"

"Well dear, it's true, Grady is a werewolf."

"I can't even."

"You just saw it. So, let's move on."

"I'm supposed to move on from the fact that werewolves exist?"

"Werewolves, shifters of other types. Bears, coyotes… I heard moose too but never met one."

"Okay, stop," I imagined what a weremoose looked like and decided the current state of things didn't need any additional imagining. I kept one eye on the road and another on Aunt Dorothy.

"And you know they all just do not get along with the trolls and forget about when the travelers start coming back. That's why Mr. Brule is here, he's got to keep the peace."

"I thought he was here to develop the ski resort?"

"Oh, for sure, that's just lovely, we need economic development in our county, and he's going to be sure that we get it! Vampires are good with investments and entrepreneurial endeavors."

"Vampires."

"Yes, let's stop being so surprised. You know, and your friends know, that Widow's Bay is legendary for our Yooper Naturals!"

"Exactly right, legend! I grew up here, and I do not remember anyone shifting into a coyote or Count Dracula terrorizing my childhood."

"Well, that's because they've been gone for decades. But now they are back, and things are as they should be."

"Gone?"

"Yes, all over the world, living their lives. But they have to come back to Widow's Bay every 75 years or so, or they will die out or be hunted or worse."

"Why do they need to be here?"

"It's the soil for the vampires. They need their home soil after a while. And for the shifters, they eventually lose control of the shift when they're not in Chippewa County. Imagine shifting while you were at the bank or a Tiger's baseball game? It's dangerous for everyone involved."

"Huh?"

"In Widow's Bay, the shifters can decide when to shift. Outside Widow's Bay, it's all about the moon and the tide, and no control whatsoever. Here's it's mostly when they want."

"Sure, yeah, that's right, I'm worried about the safety of the shifters."

"Marzie, if they can't control it eventually, they are discovered and hunted."

"Oh, right." We rolled into town, and the information was giving me a headache.

"And the dirt? You mentioned the dirt."

"Yes, the vampires have to go to ground here. I mean, they can survive a long time outside, but eventually, they need our soil."

"Can't they just have it delivered?" I was only half kidding.

"Oh, no, I mean the amount? That wouldn't make sense." I decided to roll with her explanations and pretend they were possible.

"What does Lottie Bradbury's death have to do with this?"

"Oh, she was keeping the gate closed. They can't come back unless we open the gate. She was using dark, dark magic to keep them out. It was out of spite. She had to be stopped." My Aunt's light tone got more serious. A dark thought occurred to me when she mentioned dark magic.

"Did you kill your friend?" In no way could I imagine Aunt Dorothy stabbing someone, but things were going on in this place that defied any explanation I could figure out.

"No, no, of course not." She shook her head, "Can you drop me at Elsie's? I need to check in on her. She's really not well these days."

"Yeah, she's at the assisted living place on Maple?"

"That's right, Gray Estates."

"That's an awful name for an apartment complex."

"It's quite nice. Elsie has an efficiency apartment, and the health aids check in as much or as little as you need."

"Yeah, but Gray Estates? Why didn't they just call it Death's Foyer? Whatever." I was getting sidetracked. Twenty years as a reporter and I was at a loss for what to ask next. I had a million more questions for her. I tried to organize them and found they were swirling around in my head.

"I realize you're overwhelmed, dear, but you're going to need to get over it." Aunt Dorothy looked me in the eyes. She was serious, formidable, and I reassessed whether she could have killed Lottie. Right now, she looked like she could do a damn sight more damage than any nonagenarian on the planet.

"They're all coming. Some are here, as you've seen, but all the Yooper Naturals are coming to Widow's Bay. You and your friends must fulfill the vow to them. It's your turn."

"Oh, that step up business? Well, let me tell you something, Aunt Dorothy, I'm not marrying a vampire."

"No, no. I mean, you could, but that's not the vow I'm referring to."

"What then? I didn't make any vow."

"No, but our ancestors did. We're here to be sure that the town isn't ripped apart. We're here to keep Widow's Bay safe from the inside."

"Safe? By rolling out the Welcome Wagon for werewhatevers? And bloodsuckers?"

"Right, and they'll keep us safe from the outside. There's a lot of bad stuff in the world, you've been to Detroit. You understand?"

"Ancient vows? You've got to be kidding me." I said it more to myself than to Aunt Dorothy.

"Call your friend Georgie. I know she has all the books and records and whatever it is your little journalist's brain needs."

I was ready to push her out of the car and hit the gas pedal out of here. Out of Widow's Bay, out of the U.P., out of the strange scenario I had fallen into.

"Aunt Dorothy, I didn't make any vow, and whatever you're talking about, ancestors, monsters, isn't my problem."

Aunt Dorothy unbuckled her seatbelt.

"Honey, I really should have prepared you better. I do feel bad about that. Your mother, it's her fault too. Moving to Florida never solved anything. But I'll stop pushing."

"My mother has this power or whatever?"

"No, it skips generations. Oh, it's there for your mother, but it's weak. You're strong because you're needed, and you're over 35. And single. That's key too." She rattled this off like she was listing ingredients to her recipe for lime Jell-O mold dessert.

She got out, and I watched her go up the walk to Elsie's.

I had no intention of being a hand matron to whatever was happening in this town.

None.

I leaned my head on the steering wheel.

I was supposed to meet my friends tonight at the Frog Toe. If I knew one thing, it was that I needed to connect with them. They were my touchstones, and maybe they could help me sort this out.

I wanted to know what Fawn thought, did Tatum believe what was happening, and did Georgie have something in her bookshelves that could explain any of this?

I should pick up Agnes and Bubba Smith and drive away. I shouldn't get involved.

And I thought about it. Driving immediately back over the bridge and back to civilization.

Except I was involved. I was knee-deep in something.

Something that had me curious, I had to admit that. There were so many mysteries here in Widow's Bay that my reporter's instinct was piqued. Could the legends of Widow's Bay be more than legends? Were there mystical things here that I'd sensed once before and run from?

My desire to know more won over an impulse to run away. I calmed down a notch or two. I also realized that whatever was afoot, the women in this town lived a long damn time. That was a good sign, at least.

This was my home, weird as it was. I was going to figure this out.

My phone vibrated. Justin, ugh, that's right. I still needed a story for today.

"Hey, how'd the lumber mill story go?"

I sure as hell couldn't tell him that I thought the workforce was comprised of werewolves, so I told him the least interesting component that I'd discovered today.

"No one was at the mill, but there's a bunch of new heavy equipment there. So, I'd say it's ago. I just don't have an interview or anything yet."

"Keep on it then. You need to find something for today, though."

"Yep, I'll find something. Don't worry."

I reverted to what I knew best.

Reporting.

I needed to find a story that had facts, figures, a crime even, but no shifters.

If the story were a vampire, it would have bitten me. As I rounded the corner and tried to turn onto Main Street, traffic was at a standstill.

To say there could or would ever be traffic in Widow's Bay was hilarious, really. It was a small town. If you blinked, you missed it. But whatever, traffic seemed like a nice, normal, boring, everyday story to cover. A little boring would be a welcome relief.

I pulled onto Main, and shockingly the cars were lined up, bumper to bumper in Widow's Bay.

What the heck was happening? I remembered the All Souls Festival. It was Thursday. Were people pouring in for the weekend festivities? That would be a story if nothing else. Heck, it would be a big story if frozen Widow's Bay became an actual hotspot.

I decided the best course of action would be to park here and walk up closer to figure out why there were so many cars, and why they weren't moving.

I looked at the plates of a few of the cars stuck in traffic. Michigan, New York, Ohio, Wisconsin, Indiana?

And there were ski racks on every single one.

Stephen Brule was going to have a successful opening weekend. It appeared. He'd managed to lure dozens and dozens of people to Widow's Bay.

As I walked, I took note of the way the town had decked out for the All Souls Festival idea. They'd strung lights up all the lamp poles. There was garland everywhere. Businesses welcomed visitors with new signs, and greenery in the doorways and on the awnings.

I knew they had events, a parade, a luminary candle march, a restaurant hop, and a lot more for the weekend. I'd covered it like I'd covered Halloween or Fourth of July. There was a list on the website of all the activities. But what was happening in Widow's Bay was more than a list. It was exciting. Especially in a town that couldn't catch a break in the last few decades.

Unfortunately, all the tourists who'd descended on Widow's Bay were now stuck.

Not so great for the small-town vibe if you couldn't move your car.

As I got closer, I could see exactly what was happening.

A car had crashed into a hydrant, and water was spewing from it like a geyser. I put on my reporter hat and got to work.

I took pictures and video first before anyone figured out to shut it off.

And then I got closer. The car was on its side on the sidewalk, about ten feet from the hydrant and only inches from crashing into The Broken Spine, Georgie's place.

I heard sirens. Loof and crew were on the way.

Then I saw Pauline standing next to the vehicle, she looked like she was in one piece, but it was her car.

"What in the world Pauline, are you okay?" She shook her head, and Georgie came out of her shop towards us too.

"I'm okay. I'm okay. My car? Not so much."

"What happened?"

"I got distracted." That was an understatement. Her eyes were wide, and she wasn't moving, so I moved us all further away from the water spray.

A fire truck showed up and started work on the hydrant.

"What distracted you?"

"I swear there was a bear in the intersection."

"What?"

"That's what I saw. A bear."

I looked at Georgie. "Did you see a bear?"

"Yeah, I did." She admitted.

"We need to tell Loof, they need to get the DNR."

"That's not what we need," Georgie said and gave me a pointed stare.

"Why the heck not?"

Georgie got closer and whispered in my ear.

"Because the bear is now a man and he's inside the store. I'm getting him clothes."

"Yep, what Georgie said, I thought I'd hallucinated. Phew, what a relief," Pauline said.

"We can't tell Loof that though, he'll put you in the psych ward," I said.

"Let's get inside the store. Loof will be in here soon enough," Georgie said, and we all three went inside.

"Sorry ladies, I just got in town and am working on getting the shift under control." A man with long dark hair, sparkling dark eyes, and muscles on top of muscles walked into the center of the bookstore, shirtless.

"It's okay, I just was startled," Pauline said and walked up to the bear shifting distraction.

"You're new in town. I have a lot of great properties for sale or rent. Pauline Rogers Real Estate." Pauline had shifted herself into real estate mode.

"I certainly owe you after what happened out there."

"Oh, I'm fine," Pauline said again, and amazingly she was.

Georgie stared at the giant man and appeared to be tongue-tied.

"Georgie, get him a shirt, or he's going to cause another accident," I had no doubt that most of the tourists outside could very well wrap their mini-vans around a fire hydrant if confronted with whatever this was, shirtless, in the middle of the day.

"Yeah, right, on it." She ran off to find something, and Pauline smiled politely.

"Let me get this straight, you're a bearwolf?"

"No, no, I'm a bear shifter. Totally different thing," he explained matter-of-factly.

"Sorry, my mistake."

"Common one, no worries. I was walking as me, and then I got a whiff of some awesome fish tacos."

"Oh yeah, Esther's Authentic Mexican Cuisine has them on special for lunch," Pauline explained to me.

"Anyway, you know, bears, salmon, it just took over. I got it back under control, though, super-fast! It's true what they say about Widow's Bay, so nice to be able to control it and get back to this form. Heck, anywhere else, I'd be wandering around for a few hours looking for something to eat or a place to nap!" He smiled and shook his head in amazement. Pauline and I nodded like we were commiserating like we could relate.

"Widow's Bay's the place to be, uh, I didn't catch your name?" Pauline asked, still trying to hook in a potential client it appeared.

"Bret, the name's Bret." Bret the bear shifter shook our hands, and Georgie returned with a sweatshirt.

"This is the biggest I have," Bret took it and pulled it over the muscles on top of muscles.

At that point, the front door opened, and Loof walked in.

"Pauline, I need to check you out and ask you a few questions."

"Sure, sure." She then leaned into Bret and me.

"Don't worry, I'll tell him my purse dumped over, and I looked down." She winked at Bret and walked over to Loof.

"Thanks for the shirt, and so sorry about all this. Maybe I'll see you around." Bret the Bear shrugged his broad shoulders.

"Yeah, maybe on Taco Tuesday!" I had no idea what the hell I was saying at this point. Bret walked past Loof, who appeared not to notice him at all, and out of The Broken Spine.

"This town is bananas. Ba.Nan.Aaaahz." I said to Georgie.

"Yeh, we've got a lot to talk about tonight."

"You need to dive into your local history stuff."

"Yeah?"

"We need to know why we're all of sudden Monster Town and why my Aunt thinks we need to help her and these new, uh, shifters, and well, just look up the oldest stuff you can find."

"I know just where to look. I'll bring it all tonight."

"Perfect."

I walked out of the store. The hydrant was capped off, and the police were directing a line of cars through town.

I walked back to my office and typed up a story about the influx of tourists, thanks to the All Souls Festival weekend. I added the information about the fire hydrant and the traffic tie-up.

But in the end, compared to what I'd seen today, I turned in a dull, predictable, piece, on weekend happenings, that was completely monster-free.

Even though the day had been the exact opposite.

After the story, I sat in my office and tried to process what had happened. I replayed what I'd seen in the woods.

Grady was a werewolf, and he owned an adorable puppy who'd saved my life. Or was that puppy a person too? Ugh, too many questions.

I could understand why Pauline crashed into the hydrant. Though she appeared not to be in an existential crisis like I was. She saw the bear dude as a possible client. But still, it was a shock at first, I mean she'd crashed her car. She was able to pivot faster than I was. My brain was still at war with my eyes and screaming, HE'S A BEAR SHIFTER?!

And then there was the mysterious Stephen Brule.

What did I know about Stephen Brule? In reality, very little.

He was clearly rich, handsome, and cool as the other side of the pillow. He'd invested millions in Widow's Bay and was on board with Candy's plan to turn the town into some sort of mystical tourist attraction.

If I were to believe what my eyes and my Aunt said, mystical tourism would be the perfect cover for the actual magical creatures crawling all over the place now. What did she call them? Oh yeah, Yooper Naturals. If a visitor ran into a squirrel shifter or whatever the heck was out there while they were snowshoeing, they could either write it off as a staged part of the attraction or believe they'd seen something magical.

Along with the idea of Widow's Bay as a tourist spot, it looked like Yooper Naturals were behind some of the new business. That could be big if it turned out the tourist idea was a flop. No one could deny that good, high-quality lumber was in demand. And Chippewa County had an abundance of it. Chippewa County now also had an abundance of handsome loggers. It appeared as well.

Good Lord.

Then I couldn't stop avoiding it.

I had to turn my thoughts inward, to my own inexplicable abilities, or powers, or whatever they were.

I couldn't deny that I had something extra that was magnified when I was here, and doubly so when I was with my friends. Was I supposed to use it? How was I supposed to use it? Where the heck did it come from?

If I was honest with myself, running away from Widow's Bay after high school was just as much running away from all this as it was running to a job in the big city.

I hadn't thought about any of this since I'd been gone. And now here it was in my lap, in my face, and sauntering down Main Street buck naked!

Then there was Lottie Bradbury.

Her murder had to be a part of whatever was happening in Widow's Bay.

I'd learned some things about her, but I knew there was more, hidden, out of my reach. I knew that Lottie was once much happier. A Yooper Natural disappointed her, Carlisle. He didn't save her dying brother. The woman in the picture I'd found was in love. The woman she became was all about anger.

Frances told me Aunt Dorothy, and Lottie started fighting, and if Aunt Dorothy was to be believed, Lottie was able to keep the Yooper Naturals out. I didn't know how to believe that part of the story, but I couldn't deny the fact that the moment she died, the town got mighty popular. Dorothy said it was the gate opening.

What had she done to keep it closed? And did someone kill her to open it?

Opening that gate would be a motive for killing Lottie, and that motive would point right to Aunt Dorothy and her monster boyfriends.

I put my head in my hands, Dottie and The Monster Boyfriends sounded like an excellent name for a rock band.

I wondered if Loof had any leads yet.

I recounted the actual clues I'd scrounged up. I'd found that Lottie had a list of the dads who'd died in the bus crash. Ominous, weird, but it only proved Lottie was nutty. Or maybe someone else thought Lottie was plotting against the dads?

I pulled up the photos I'd taken of the crime scene. There were footprints in the fresh snow, but those were from the UPS guy. I did a quick search and found that the footprints matched a standard Rockport Workboot. It looked like Loof was right on that score.

Was money a motive? Nothing was stolen from her home, according to police, and nothing looked particularly disturbed, other than Lottie.

None of the roads lead to an answer, and all of them led to more forks.

I put the Lottie Bradbury murder aside.

Before I left for the day, I decided to take one more look at the other story I'd uploaded for Your U.P. News. The security video of the snowmobile crashing into Holiday Gas was doing great on the website. I watched it again.

Something was bothering me about it, but I couldn't figure out what. No one had identified the helmet wearing, cig stealing bandit, but they were watching.

I played the video a few more times. It was the number one video on the entire Your U.P. News website. The number two most popular story on the site was my exclusive with Stephen Brule.

Well, that was some good news. I was earning my keep in web traffic at my new job.

Despite the bizarre universe I was trying to sort out, I could still turn a good story without magic or vampires. That made me feel a tad bit better about the craziness.

I decided one last call to Loof for the day made sense.

He picked up fast.

"Hey Loof, bet you thought you'd never see a traffic jam in Downtown Widow's Bay?"

"You know it. And Councilman Schutte was in here yelling up a storm. He blames Councilwoman Hitchcock, oh what did he call it? Oh yes, her aggressive whoring out of the town to business interests."

"Sort of an overreaction to our first ever traffic jam, don't you think?"

"Yeah, uh, wait, don't quote me, Chief Marvin will have my head!"

"No, no, just talking with you. I do have a few quick follow-ups."

"I'm off the clock."

"No, it's 4:55, you have five more minutes, and I'll only take one."

"Alright."

"Anything new with Lottie Bradbury?"

"We released her body to the mortuary, and services are set for tomorrow, I think."

"Who's handling it?"

"Sukulski's, of course."

I resolved to attend the visitation for Lottie Bradbury. Maybe something there would shed light on who killed her.

"Anything new in the case? Suspects? Witnesses? There has to be something."

"There's one thing, but it's really not much. Elsie Faulkner was seen walking in the neighborhood kind of late, the night Lottie died. Her home called the department and said she'd wandered off. One of her DLC biddies picked her up and brought her back."

"Elsie's a suspect? The woman is addled and probably weighs 100 pounds."

"No, not a suspect, but maybe she saw something?"

"Hmm. Okay, that's something. Your challenge will be getting her to reliably remember anything after 1960. What about the snowmobile thief?"

"We had a few folks call in and identify who they thought it was."

"And?"

"They were wrong. Every single one had an alibi, so that case is still open. And that darn Todd Bialecki's still complaining about his helmet even though we got him his snowmobile back. Some people are never happy."

"That's true. I'll let you go, Loof. See, I only took up one minute."

"I appreciate that Marzie have a good night."

"You too, Loof."

I called it a day.

I had to meet with my friends and, of course, had a cauldron to get to.

CHAPTER 14

I checked in at home after work. Agnes strolled in to greet me, not her normal modus operandi.

I hope you plan to work on this house. Not a fan of the décor.

Great, she'd moved on from criticizing my wardrobe to assessing the HGTV worthiness of the place.

"That is not a top priority."

Which was the truth. Part of me would love to invest time, creative energy, and actual energy turning this Victorian around. It hadn't been updated since I was a kid, and my mom brought in awful eighties trends when she did update. There were mauve accents that had to go.

I could picture myself doing the research, cleaning the fixtures, exposing hardwood under the carpet, and finding antiques to fill the place.

I loved the idea of making the house mine. The truth was I didn't really think I was staying. Whatever obligations my Aunt claimed I had were in her head. I didn't make a vow to this town. I'd made a vow to try to pick up the pieces after my kids went to college, and my husband went to Kayleigh Carson.

Still, I had to admit, I loved the old house and the neighborhood. No one built houses like this anymore. The walls were plaster, and the baseboards were six inches high. The house was built with charming little nooks and expansive spaces for dining.

It's had enormous potential. It was an HGTV addict's dream. Agnes and Bubba had fit right into this new place. They had their favorite cozy cubbies and didn't seem to miss the chaos of life with two sons and a husband.

Still, the shaky ground I'd felt myself on before I'd come home to Widow's Bay was nothing compared to the rocking and rolling landscape of the last few days.

Adding shiplap or exposing wood floors wasn't on my to-do list right now. Keeping one foot, in reality, was taking up all my available time and attention.

I checked myself in the mirror. Was I still me? After all, I'd been forced to see today? Did I see the same person in the mirror?

I guess I looked the same, but a streak of gray that I'd been covering looked more prominent. Had all this talk of vampires and monsters actually turned me into Lily Munster? The swath of steel in my dark hair seemed to glow from root to end.

I ran a brush through my mop. I swiped a bit of fresh lip gloss on and called myself ready. Agnes could stuff it; it was all the grooming I had time for.

The meeting of the not so distinguished ladies of Widow's Bay was about to begin.

The cauldron was waiting.

There were six of us dialed into this little get together. Tatum, of course, Fawn, and Georgie. But we also included Pauline and Candy, since they were deep into whatever was going on too.

I wasn't BFFs with Candy or Pauline, but in some combination of three, with me and without me, all six of us had experienced something extra. From psychic communication to premonitions to bare-naked bear men jaywalking around Main Street.

I had to park rather far away from the Frog Toe. Apparently, All Souls weekend was in full swing on a Thursday night. Widow's Bay was downright packed.

I walked into the Frog Toe and wondered if it had been a wise choice. I couldn't exactly hear myself think much less figure out the mysteries of the universe.

I made my way to the cauldron, and our spots were all taken by the Hoopsters and tourists as Tatum named them.

Tatum found me, though.

"Marzie." We hugged, and she looked at my gray streak and shook her head.

"I know you're skeptical as hell about what's going on around here, but can you believe this? Quiet little Widow's Bay? At this rate, I'm going to pay off the house by the end of the year!"

"I have never seen it like this, that's for sure. Are the rest of the girls here?"

"Yes, and sorry, I can't spare valuable cauldron space, I've got us in a quieter back room, that work?"

"Sounds perfect."

"Let me tell the bar manager I'm off the floor. The room's right there." She pointed to a wall that had several alcoves separated by windowed doors. You could close them off for private parties or open them up on a busy night like this.

I was the last to arrive. Georgie had a box of papers and books, Candy was taking some urgent call or another, Pauline was texting furiously. Fawn was the only one not otherwise occupied and patted the seat next to her. I walked over and sat.

"Tatum's on the way in, I'm surprised she can get away at all with the level of the crowd here today." Candy had ended her call.

"Exactly, we're pumping real money into Widow's Bay's businesses. How Ridge continues to fight this is beyond me," Candy said.

"He wasn't too thrilled about the little traffic jam today," I relayed the information but spared Candy the details of his outburst.

"And it's seasonal? He doesn't get that we'll have surges in October, Christmas, and of course, mid-summer. We're already planning Imbolc, Beltane, and Lughnasadh festivals. We have to work on some catchier names yet, but it's going to keep drawing people in like this! Ridge is going to have to get his head out of the snow." Candy explained that the meetings and committees were already "tasked" with making each festival work.

Tatum came in and closed the glass door. It was surprisingly effective in muting the noise of the crowded micro-brewery. "So not only are we having an influx of tourists, the word's out about Keno Stout," Tatum said, and she sat down on Marzie's other side.

"Yeah, you need to limit that to a special reserve," Fawn knew about casinos. You didn't mess with the odds by counting cards or casting spells if you wanted to keep on this side of iron bars or boxes.

"I think it works for luck in tourism marketing. We brought a sample to the Michigan Chamber of Commerce last year when we announced the Widow's Bay rebrand and booyah! It's working. I sold three houses today and had more calls about rentals than I could take!" If a person could dance while sitting, Pauline was doing it.

"Wow," Georgie said.

"Yeah, we weren't looking so good as a tourist attraction after the bus crash. No one wants to visit a town whose claim to fame is tragic death and grieving widows." Candy's deadpan delivery belied the fact that it was one-hundred percent true.

But that might have also contributed to what was going on. Haunted small town? Maybe that was an appeal?

"You're so lucky you're divorced, you can complain about Sam. You don't know what it's been like. Now that we're widows, we've got to remember sainted Darius Rogers. Or God Rest

Larry Hitchcock's soul. It's kind of oppressive. I mean, Darius used to clip his nails in the kitchen, but now he's The Sainted Darius."

Mourning didn't become Pauline, and neither did wallowing. It was true. When you added the label widow, you were supposed to be sainted, vaunted, and perennially pitied. None of my friends wanted anyone to feel sorry for them over anything.

Though finding your husband in a compromising position didn't exactly seem like a great option either.

"Oh, yes, I'm very lucky. Look, we need to get to the topic at hand," I said.

"Agree. I've got a night meeting." Candy was always going one meeting to another. That sounded like a version of hell to me.

"Let's compare notes. Fawn and I saw a wolf turn into a man, we also had a psychic communication when I thought I was about to be wolf kibble," I relayed the incident in the woods. And they all unbelievably believed me.

"Georgie and I saw a giant bear turn into a man, a naked man, who had a great butt," Pauline said.

"Most of us were here when that bar fight froze in mid-air and a vampire, I think he's a vampire, a Viking one. Or maybe he's French? Anyway, we can all agree he cooled everyone's jets," Tatum recounted our weird freeze-frame moment, "Oh, and I'm ninety-percent sure that the bouncer that Brule sent over here is also a vampire."

"Oh my God," I felt my eyes pop wide open.

"No, he's pretty good, helped me catch a busboy who was stealing from the bartender tip jar, and he has a delicious recipe for Bloody Marys. I think I caught him sneaking a whiff of my neck, and he can't pull lunch shifts, daytime is a no go. But I'm still coming out ahead," Tatum said.

"Glad to see you're unphased by possible bloodsucking." I tried not to roll my eyes. Then I turned to Candy.

"Candy, how about you?" I pointed the question at her

because she was the last one to admit magic, mystical, or even give in to a hair out of place.

"Hmm, well, I have had that step-up dream like you were mentioning." That meant we all had it. I wondered if it was just us six or other women in Widow's Bay had it too.

"Oh, and Mary Jo Navarre and I were leaving City Hall last night, and Dwight Lapeer was raving about Maxine cursing his chickens, said all the eggs were rotten this week. He's always asking for formal police intervention on something, so I don't know if you put the eggs in the magical category or mark it down as general litigiousness."

"Mary Jo, does she have the dreams? Do we all?"

"Not sure, I mean, we are probably special," Pauline said with a wink.

"Aunt Dorothy said we had to fulfill a vow. That we owed some sort of debt, so I had Georgie do some research," I wanted to get to the bottom of why Aunt Dorothy thought it was our duty to do, well, I didn't know what she wanted me to do.

I had said no, but I was curious to know why she thought I had no choice in the matter.

"Yeah, I found some documents that are quite frankly incredible." Georgie leaned forward and opened a gigantic book filled with yellowing pages. "These are the oldest documents I can find about our area."

Pauline reached out to touch one, and Georgie put a hand out to stop her.

"No, we shouldn't handle them too much, they'll fall apart. I digitized what I could. Here."

Georgie broke out her iPad and fired it up.

"This one is the charter." I leaned forward to try to read the scanned in copy. It was titled Le Griffon Compact.

"Who's Le Griffon?" I asked.

"I had to look that up too. I'd never heard of it. But get a load of this. Le Griffon was the first full-sized sailing ship on the upper Great Lakes of North America, and she led the way to modern commercial shipping in our neck of the woods. It's also considered the first shipwreck because no one knows what happened to it. No one's ever found where she sunk exactly. It's like the Holy Grail of Great Lakes Shipwrecks."

"So Compact, that's an agreement, like The Mayflower Compact," Candy weighed in on what we were trying to decipher.

"Exactly," Georgie replied.

We dove into the arcane language of Le Griffon Compact.

Le Griffon Compact

In ye own name Amen· We whose names are vnderwriten,
The loyall subjects of our dread soueraigne Lord King James
By ye grace of God, of Great Britaine, Franc, Ireland king, and savage kingdoms of the new west.

Having vndertaken as loyal servants we of ye Christian faith and honour of our king & countrie, a voyage to plant ye first colonie in ye Western parts of New France·

Do hereby these presents solemnly & mutually in ye presence of the sky, and one of another, covenant, & combine our selves together into a binding body; for ye our better ordering, & preseruation & furtherance of ye ends aforesaid; and by virtue hereof, to enact a constitute, and frame such just & equal laws.

The founders have with the protection and aid of the Frenchman, escaped their unjust imprisonment and may now live as freewomen bound to repay the debt in perpetuity.

For our own soveignty, we shall marry to the sky, the creature, the blood, the earth and the spirit.

We shall cultivate the land and its bounty and from time to time draft Acts, constitutions, & offices, as shall be thought most meet & convenient for ye generall good of ye colony of New France:

Unto the four aforementioned we promise all due submission and obedience in exchange for the protection of our lands and kin in perpetuity. We promise to protect the lines using the powers and gifts from sky, the creature, the blood, the earth and the spirit.

In witness whereof, we have hereunder subscribed our names at Gros Rocher.

August – 1693
Abigail Faulkner
Mary Bradbury
Sarah Corey
Mercy Parris
Lydia Proctor
Susannah Nurse
Isabeau LaFramboise

"THERE ARE THIRTEEN NAMES, but I can only make out the seven," Georgie said.

"What does it mean?" Pauline asked. I was about as mystified as she was. The language was English, but barely. Candy spoke up on this one.

"It really is an agreement."

"The names," I looked again at the signatures, all the names we could read were familiar.

"Right, that's the crazy part. All of the names are names that are still in this town. Hell, they're names in our own family trees," Georgie said.

I may be Marzie Nowak, but my mother's name was Nurse. Fawn had LaFramboise relatives. And Candy Hitchcock had changed her name from Faulkner when she got married to Larry.

Georgie showed us a few more founding documents, survey maps, basic legal tenants, and generally difficult to read official paperwork of the founding of Widow's Bay.

"The weird thing is the number of women who sign and vote on things. That's unheard of in old documents," Georgie said.

"Yeah, I was noticing that too," Candy clicked through the names again.

"For the love of Susan B. Anthony, we didn't even get the vote until 1920. And this says the town elders, the signers of a bunch of this stuff, were all women?" I wasn't a historian but could see the importance and uniqueness of that bit of historical fact.

"And they're all co-signed by one person," Georgie pointed to a larger, more florid signature.

"What's the name, I can't really make it out," Tatum said.

"Almost everything is witnessed or certified by Etienne Brule," Georgie said and let it sit there.

"OH MY GOD! No way! Could it be Stephen Brule's like great-great-great-grandfather or something?" Tatum said.

"Add about ten more greats," I said.

"Yeah, or none. Etienne is translated as Stephen," Fawn said.

"You're saying the Stephen Brule in town now is actually legendary explorer Etienne Brule?" The numbers here were unworkable. Unbelievable.

Georgie's eyes were wide and there was a smile of excitement on her lips.

"I'm willing to open up to a lot of things, but that would put him at four-hundred years old," I felt a headache trying to erupt behind my left eye.

"Paleo diet I bet," Pauline nodded her head like she'd discovered that the fountain of youth was avoiding gluten and dairy.

"Or just undead and doing CrossFit," Tatum said to Pauline and both looked thrilled by the prospect. I was having a harder time seeing the humor.

"This is all ancient, ridiculous, and holds about as much legal water as a slotted serving spoon," I said.

"There's one more wrinkle," Georgie said and pulled up a Wikipedia page. The heading read Salem Witch Trials.

"Oh no, that's just, no. We're not going there are we?" I asked, but I knew the answer.

"We're going there and, in a handbasket," Georgie said. "Quite a few of the names on there are linked to the Salem Witch Trials. They're family names of women who historians believe were accused but escaped Salem during the witch trials."

We all sat in silence.

"Don't you think our moms would have told us this stuff? Why is it the first we're hearing about it now?" We'd all lived here our whole lives except my defection to Detroit. But we certainly all grew up here. I thought about the skipping of the generations that Dorothy said happened.

"Well we all know the ghost stories," Pauline said.

"And I for one am not running a campaign for mayor based on witchcraft and wizardry, it's tourism and industry," Candy said and straightened her suit jacket.

"Except we did serve the Keno Stout at the Michigan Chamber of Commerce thing," Pauline pointed out and Candy reluctantly nodded.

"Look, if we're honest, we knew we had powers," Georgie said, and she was right.

I hated to admit it. I'd tried to avoid it, and I'd run from it. It was right in front of my eyes now no matter how hard I tried to squeeze them shut.

There was no denying the world as I knew it was not the world as I knew it.

The reporter in me also wondered about the rules, who were affected by them, why? My curiosity piqued on so many fronts. The women in this room clearly saw something extra, but did everyone in town?

"There's more here to dig through after the founding of the town. Genealogy, sightings of people reported missing, I didn't know exactly what we needed," Georgie said.

"You did amazing finding this stuff. We've got a lot to sort through, and we're not going to be able to do it in one night. What about the ages of the Distinguished Ladies? They can't really be as old as they say?" I was sure they had to be lying about being 97 or older.

"I looked up the birth records of Dorothy Nurse, Lottie Bradbury, and Jane Parris," Georgie said and let it hang there for a moment.

"Well?" Candy pushed her. The woman did have another meeting.

"As far as I could tell, they were all born before 1919."

"Jesus, Mary and Joseph," Candy said.

"Or good Botox," Pauline said.

We had unearthed a box full of answers that raised a mountain's worth of questions.

But I was a reporter. Questions were my business.

CHAPTER 15

I started my Friday with a quick call to my boys at school. We discussed how to wash jeans, what I could send them in the next care package, and a question about whether they could move from the dorms to Cedar Village apartments. They asked how I was and were fine with my answer of, fine. They didn't need to know a thing about anything, in my opinion. How could I get them up to speed on anything if I was so confused?

And it had been my experience that they were good if they thought I was safe and said I was happy. My problems didn't need to be their worries.

I spent most of Friday reading the town's history from Georgie, taking care of chores I'd neglected in my frenzied first week here, and trying to gather my thoughts.

Soon enough, it was time to head to Lottie Bradbury's visitation.

I decided to dress up for the first time since moving back to Widow's Bay.

I'd donated just about every single stitch of brightly hued

anchorwoman wear. I kept a few classic suits, black pumps, and quality blouses. But a very few.

Wearing hose, tucking in a blouse, and worse, squeezing into three-inch heels was part of my daily uniform at WXYD. I didn't realize how much it had restricted me until I was free of it for a few days.

Jeans, turtlenecks, and boots had been a little piece of heaven for the last few days and had become a surprising benefit to this change in my life. Candy Hitchcock dressed like she could be tapped to walk a Presidential Inaugural Parade at a moment's notice. But everyone else in Widow's Bay kept their own casual style with their own tricks on how not to freeze to death.

But for the Visitation of Lottie Bradbury, I donned a classic Calvin Klein blazer, pencil skirt, and crisp white blouse. I slid my feet into the pumps and checked the outfit situation in the mirror before I head out.

Finally. I was getting so embarrassed for you. Maybe you can salvage what you've done to your chance with that burly Brule character with this look.

Agnes yawned in my direction.

"I'm not interested in finding a date. I'm going to the visitation of an elderly woman who was murdered."

Whatever. You've got lipstick on your teeth.

Agnes for the win. She knew it and sauntered out of my bedroom. I smoothed my hair and, for good measure, added my string of real pearls. My mother had given them to me when I graduated high school. The pearls hadn't seen studio lights in years because understated read old on television. One of the many bits of advice I'd been given by news consultants over the years.

Screw them all.

I drove to the Sukulski Funeral Home. It was the only game in town if you died.

The place had done big business a few years ago when the bus crash happened, and I had to admit they did a great job handling media requests for pictures of the deceased.

That's what no one expects when tragedy strikes. Someone from the media is going to be asking for a picture or an interview at a moment when the unthinkable has happened.

Many times, I was the person asking.

I'd been asked, how could I do it? How could I approach someone in the throes of grief and ask for an interview or a snapshot?

Here's how: carefully, and respectfully. And with the mindset that the loved one is now silent, they can no longer tell their story. It's up to the family, friends, parents to do it, and it's up to me, the reporter.

So, I asked, and then crafted a story, always mindful that the voice I was trying to convey had been silenced. That's how I could ask. Because I viewed telling the stories of those, who couldn't as a sacred trust, not a torrid ploy.

Sukulski's had handled requests for photos back when the bus crash happened, they let the media know where and what to shoot for our news stories. I respected their professionalism.

This time I didn't have a camera or a need to get sound bites. I wanted to be respectful of Lottie and maybe see if anyone revealed themselves as happy she was gone.

Sukulski's had been in operation as long as I could remember. My father had died of a heart attack when I was 13, and Sukulski's handled the arrangements. Those days are a blur, but I do remember Emil Sukulski, the owner and undertaker, being nice to me. He'd set me up in a TV room so I could watch General Hospital when I was overwhelmed with the expectation of people's sympathy.

The funeral home was set up to look like a home, to make you feel as comfortable as you could in the worst situation. It had a massive foyer with a staircase that led to the offices upstairs and a chandelier that sparkled in the center of the room. Sukulski's had six rooms available for families to gather. When the football dads had died, the line of mourners waiting to pay respects stretched to the parking lot. Not so much for Lottie Bradbury.

Emil Sukulski was there, at the guest book, and he greeted me with a warm smile of recognition. Mr. Sukulski was a slight man. He was always perfectly groomed and neat. His welcoming disposition was incredible, given what he did for a living. Or maybe that's why he was perfect for doing what he did for a living.

"I'd heard you were back in Widow's Bay. Such good news for us all." The man had kind eyes, and I was glad to see him. I guess when your business is death, you either turn bitter and cynical or dip into a deep well of something good. Emil had faith. His faith had been a steady arm to lean on for a lot of people, including the teenaged me.

"That's very sweet."

He hugged me. It was the part of living in a small town that I had missed. I'd missed it and didn't recognize it as such until these last few years. Mr. Sukulski handed me a pen to sign the guestbook. I wrote my signature and then scanned the names. It was a shortlist.

"I'll be saying a few prayers around seven."

"No pastor or priest here?"

"She was a loner these last few decades."

"Who made the arrangements?"

"Out of towner," Emil slyly pointed to the guest book and the signature. It read Carlisle Brule. I wondered how this particular Brule was related. Carlisle was the name of Lottie's old beau.

"Paid too," Emil whispered to me, and I cocked my head. I would have thought her nephew would be the one to handle things. But as I walked into the parlor on the left of the foyer and looked around, I did not see the nephew. Or a man who looked like he could be the one I'd seen with Lottie in the picture.

I did see Byron DeLoof chatting up Chief Marvin in a corner.

There were a few familiar faces I'd recognized from her neighborhood too.

I did see the full contingent of Distinguished Ladies. They were sitting, chatting, and I had to say they looked tense.

"Is that really us in 50 years?" It was Georgie. She'd come too, followed by Pauline, Candy, Tatum, and Fawn. She was looking at the Distinguished Ladies.

"Can we be called something else? Like All the Single Ladies?" I quipped.

"Better," Tatum said.

"Let's go up and pay our respects." Candy said, and we filed up to the casket, which was closed. I supposed that it was a very good thing based on how she'd died.

We all took turns kneeling.

I sent up a prayer that I would be resourceful enough to find out what happened to Lottie, and I prayed to be empathetic enough to tell her story. And I prayed that her soul, clearly one that was not content in life, found peace.

I stood and made way for Candy, who took a spot in front of the casket and kneeled. I was always reminded of a blonde Jackie O when Candy did something like this. She channeled that same stoic, official glamour I'd seen in old photos of the First Lady.

A line of new attendees entered. And they were not like the others. They were some of the new faces we'd seen in Widow's Bay. Grady, the shifter I'd encountered in the woods, entered with a rough-hewn group of men that were clearly the lumber-jack contingent of mourners.

Then Stephen Brule appeared with his handsome crew of well-dressed vampires-- shoot, no. They weren't vampires. Was I really accepting this? That a group of vampire mourners was there in Sukulski's?

This strange reality was somehow becoming normal in my head.

I realized that any time I'd seen our new neighbors in close proximity to one another, things had devolved into a brawl.

I watched as the Lumberjacks led by Grady, walked up to my Aunt Dorothy. She smiled, and so did the other Distinguished ladies. Each man nodded and paid respects to the older women, then moved along though to a far corner of the room and sat down.

This made way for the Europeans. Stephen Brule made eye contact with me. I felt a shiver run up and down my spine. He broke eye contact and then led about six of them to Aunt Dorothy, Elsie, Maxine, and Frances. This time they kissed the hands of the old bats.

The EuroVamps also headed to a neutral corner of the large room, and that gave me hope that we might get through this memorial service without fists, fangs, or fur flying.

But at that moment, a shriek cut through the muted conversation and soft music of the room.

I whipped around to see Candy Hitchcock standing in front of Lottie's coffin, her hands were on it, fingers splayed wide.

"You, you. YOU! YOU KILLED HIM. YOU KILLED ALL OF THEM. YOU SELFISH WITCH. IT WAS YOU!!!!" Candy was shaking. I'd never seen so much as an eyelash out of control on her, and she'd come unhinged!

I rushed to her side. Her eyes were wide, like an animal cornered.

Fawn ran to her other side, and Pauline wasn't far behind.

"Candy step back," I didn't know how I knew, but I knew that touching that casket was the conduit for whatever she was feeling and saying.

"Somehow, she killed them, that crash… it was her," Candy's perfectly composed self was gone. Her hair escaped its coiffed blow out, and curls sprung around her face.

"Honey, it's okay. Let's take a minute," Pauline said. I looked over to Emil, and he nodded to the room I'd chilled out in so many decades ago.

Fawn and Pauline supported a shocked Candy.

As we did, of course, Ridge Schutte walked in, took a good look at Candy, and then walked over to Chief Marvin. Trying to good ole boy it up, I supposed.

"This is exactly why," he said loudly to Chief Marvin. "A woman like that should not be mayor, she needs help and rest."

Tatum decided to handle the Ridge situation.

"Shove it, Schutte, or I'll share on Facebook that little secret, you know I know," Tatum said to Ridge. I had no idea what she was talking about, but he shut up.

That was good. Candy didn't need campaign shenanigans right now. She needed to sort herself out.

We got Candy situated in the room designated for family members to pop in and rest during a long day of services or visitation. There was a fridge, a TV, a couch, whatever you might need to collect yourself for a little while. Fawn grabbed a water from the fridge and handed it to Candy, who was sitting on the couch.

"I, ugh. Ridge saw me, right? Any other voters?" Candy was pulling herself back together and starting to assess the damage her outburst might have caused to her campaign.

"Don't worry about it. Tatum put him in his place, and the rest of them were mostly the new hot dudes of the month," Pauline said.

"Yeah, they can't have registered to vote yet," Georgie spoke Candy's language for a second. She nodded in agreement that she probably hadn't lost any votes. It was always in her mind, it appeared.

"What did you mean?" I asked Candy.

"It was the casket. It started it, right? It talked to you somehow?" Fawn had come to the same conclusion I had.

"Yes, I saw as clear as if I was in her house. She was making some stew or something, a soup, I guess, and whatever she was doing was causing the weather. She was saying words about the bus about the bridge. She did it. She made that bus crash happen. She brewed up the storm." Candy said, and Fawn nodded.

"We need to talk to the Distinguished Ladies. They know what's what," Fawn said.

"You're right. Let's finish this visitation, and then we grill those Crones," I proposed.

"Yes, yes," Candy said.

"You want to chill in here while Sukulski does his thing?" Pauline asked.

"No, I need to show that I've not lost my mind. It was a momentary grief-stricken breakdown. I'm fine. I need to show that." And Candy was fine. She was pulling herself back together as fast as she'd come apart.

She stood up and smoothed her hair. We all flanked her, and she led us back out into the parlor.

There were a few looks, but it was as if it hadn't happened.

We sat down in the row of folding chairs that Emil had set up, and the Distinguished Ladies, the EuroVamps, and the lumber-jacks all did the same. The first few rows were open, and the few neighbors or acquaintances filled those places in.

Emil Sukulski walked up to the lectern and began his speech.

"We're gathered here this evening to say a few prayers for the immortal soul of Charlotte Bradbury."

We all put our heads down. I had to wonder, though, if Charlotte Bradbury's soul was in Heaven or rotting in hell.

After Candy's outburst, I put money on the second scenario.

CHAPTER 16

*T*he services ended quickly. Emil knew how to read an audience. No one here wanted to sit for an hour listening to a generic eulogy.

I realized I'd left my purse in the resting room after he finished speaking.

I broke away from the group to retrieve it. On my way back to the main parlor while still hidden from view of anyone in the hallway, I heard voices. And I froze.

I knew exactly who the voices belonged to, and they were in deep conversation near the coat rack. I did my best to listen in.

Aunt Dorothy was talking to Stephen Brule.

"We're sorry for flooding the town so quickly. You know that's the source of some of the unrest. Too much too fast. It couldn't be avoided."

I figured he was talking about all the new monsters that had decided to move into our zip code.

"It was our fault. I couldn't fight against her."

"Her actions affected gateways on all the continents. They all remained closed."

"Oh, my. I'm so sorry about that. You know Lottie, or at least your brother did. She was stubborn and held a grudge."

"Yes. Well. You need to get the young ones up to speed, or this will get worse."

"I've tried. They are very modern… you know if it's not on Facebook, it can't be true," Dorothy said to Brule.

"We're not going anywhere, and if you want some manner of peace in this town, we're going to need help. It's what we have all worked for, Dorothy."

"I know. I'll work on them. They'll come around."

"And thank you finally doing what you had to do to open the gate. It couldn't have been easy. She was a friend once."

"Once. Yes," Dorothy said.

Everything was just outside of my understanding. I was close to the answer to a puzzle, but pieces were missing. Their conversation clarified things and confused me at the same moment.

"It had to be done. She was the true monster. Don't fret," Brule said to Dorothy.

"But I…" And the rest was muffled. I peeked around the corner, and he saw me.

Brule had my Aunt in a comforting embrace, and his eyes were on me.

"Marzenna, you need to have some family time with your Aunt." He said, and she stepped back and turned to look at me.

"Yes, oh, dear. Yes." I didn't stop looking at Brule.

"Then we need to talk, perhaps over a nightcap," Brule said.

"A nightcap? Who says nightcap?" Because really, who did?

"Is that not correct?" He looked at me with an amused smile.

"It's correct if you're in the 1950s or something." I rolled my eyes at both of them and walked past them.

"Emil, can we borrow the family area for a little while?" I asked our gracious host. It was time to get to the bottom of this, whatever this was.

"Certainly. Just knock on my door when you leave so I can

lock up." Emil was folding chairs and straightening his parlor. A curtain had been drawn around the casket. Pauline, Fawn, Tatum, Georgie, and Candy were waiting.

I pointed to them and the rest of the older women.

"We're meeting in the comfort room now. All of us."

Aunt Dorothy was behind me, and her crew did what I asked.

"Yes, it's about time," she said in case they were planning not to listen to me.

The Yooper Natural types had taken off, and it appeared Ridge, and the rest of mourners were also gone.

It would be just The Crones and us.

We all filed into the resting room, the younger ladies giving seats to the older. There were ten of us packed in there, which was just about capacity.

"This isn't the best place for a meeting, but we can't put it off any longer. Just not a moment longer," Aunt Dorothy said.

"I'm tired, that's for sure," Maxine said, and Elsie nodded.

"Me too. Be quick. I've got a show to watch at nine. Shark Tank." Frances added her two cents.

Aunt Dorothy rubbed her nose and looked exasperated with her friends. I suppose if they were all friends for nearly one-hundred years, you would get peevish now and then.

"Ladies, we've held our tongues long enough. As you've all been messaged. It's time for you to step up."

"Ugh, not that again." Candy was back to normal, and I agreed with her sentiment.

"We've all been stepping up as far as I can see. Candy is a public servant. Tatum, Pauline, and Georgie run successful businesses, even in a crappy economy. Fawn is taking care of everyone's pets and their neurotic owners. Just what do you want from these women?" I was as peevish as Aunt Dorothy at this point.

"Specifically, I can't say for them. But for you? Well, that's been obvious," Aunt Dorothy said to me, and I shook my head.

"She's resistant, that's what's obvious. Thinks she's too cool,"

Maxine said, and I looked at her like she was speaking a foreign language.

"She did move away. That's never good," Frances piped in. I put my hand up to stop their banter. I needed answers, not banter.

"Enough. What the hell's going on in this town?" I asked point-blank, and I knew my voice revealed all the frustration and confusion I felt.

"She thought we were the ones with dementia," Maxine said out the corner of her mouth, but loudly, to Elsie.

"To be fair, Elsie put a loaf of bread in the dryer instead of the toaster this morning," Frances countered.

"That didn't work at all," Elsie chimed in, she'd been distracted by the fluffed not toasted loaf of bread, instead of focusing on the issue at hand.

"Enough," Aunt Dorothy put a hand up, just like I had, but this time the other three quieted down. I looked at my group and saw a fair amount of amusement at the direction or lack of it in this impromptu meeting.

"Marzenna, Fawn, Candy, Tatum, Pauline, and Georgie—ha, see I remember all the names, dementia my bum! Anyway, all of you young ladies need to listen up right now." Aunt Dorothy put on her best stern voice.

"We're all ears," Tatum said.

"I have questions, and you're going to give me some non-insane answers," I added.

Aunt Dorothy narrowed her eyes at that comment and cleared her throat.

"Widow's Bay owes the Yooper Naturals sanctuary, protection, and whatever else they may need. How's that for answers?" Aunt Dorothy said.

"How are there even Yooper Naturals? Werewolves or shifters or vampires, that's insane," I said.

"Well, you've seen them with your own eyes," Elsie piped up.

And Fawn decided to add to that observation.

"It's true, she has, she's just the most rigid of all of us." This was coming from Fawn. I bristled at the assessment. I always thought Candy was the most uptight.

"Okay fine. There are Yooper Naturals or whatever you want to call what we've seen. And fine, we've all seen strange stuff. And it's getting stranger, but I fail to see what we, any of us, have to do with this."

"We read the old charter," Georgie directed her comment at Aunt Dorothy.

"Good, good. So, let me just sum up. Your ancestors from way back and not so way back all owes them," Aunt Dorothy said.

"What do we owe? I hate working on credit," Tatum spoke up.

"Well, that's the tricky part. Marzenna, you will be Brule's eyes and ears in town. You'll be The Liaison for him. Very important, and that's the one duty I can figure pretty clearly from how the last few days have gone," Aunt Dorothy said.

"Excuse me." I felt a headache coming on.

"Let me back up. Our ancestors founded this town, and if you read the documents, you know we come from a strong line of witches. Witches who escaped Salem, and some who got the heck out of Europe too."

"Escaped thanks to Brule and his lot," Maxine said.

"They got our great great great greats OUT of Salem, then they traveled here. It was remote and safe from the rest of the world. The Yooper Naturals also helped ensure that the women were allowed to do whatever they wanted in Widow's Bay."

"That answers that suffragette question," Georgie said. She'd pointed out that the town was predominantly guided by women, as far back as records were kept.

"That's right, women in Widow's Bay always had a say, a vote, control over their own bodies. The Yoopers helped keep the rest of the world out until the rest of the world caught up with us, with the vote and birth control and whatnot." Aunt Dorothy had reduced equal rights to "what not" apparently.

"But nothing's free, that's what you, hashtag, girl boss, types don't quite grasp," Frances, who'd been mostly quiet during this little confab added with some annoyance. She made a hashtag sign with her hands when she said it.

"Nothing is free, that's right. We got a perfect place to live our lives, control our lives. In exchange, well, they need this town. Every 75 or so years, they need it if they're going to survive," Aunt Dorothy said.

"And we want vampires to survive because?" I stated the obvious. They were evil, right? I mean, Brule didn't seem evil. Dangerous yes, evil no.

"If they don't go to ground in our county or the shifters don't get back to home base here, they die out or lose control of the shift. And you can imagine how hunted they'd be then. We covered this dear," Aunt Dorothy said.

"Vampires drink blood, werewolves, uh, bite? I have no idea what the other monsters you mentioned do, but aren't we talking evil here?"

"Oh, they're just like us, except better looking and have lower cholesterol," Frances said.

"Well, just like us in that some are decent, and some are asshats," Maxine dropped the word asshat. An involuntary chuckle came out of my mouth.

Aunt Dorothy got very serious all of a sudden and looked me in the eyes. The old lady in her dotage façade was dropped, and the air felt different. Silently she commanded the space. The chatter stopped.

"Make no mistake. They may not be evil, but they are dangerous. But the danger works for us. And we work for them. And we work together against those who'd seek Widow's Bay for themselves."

What now?

"Doing what?" I still had no idea what this really meant, how my friends and I were supposed to pay a debt that we didn't rack up.

"Each of you will find out in good time, in your own way, what's required, but you, Marzenna, you're the connection between Brule and the town. Every single time there's been a dust-up between the different factions that are arriving, you've summoned him," Aunt Dorothy said.

"I most certainly didn't summon anyone." I thought back over the last few days.

"I think you did," Tatum said.

"The bar fight, the fight outside of cycling class, even your wolf encounter. I totally heard you in the woods." Fawn listed the incidents, and I shook my head.

"You broke up the fight outside of cycling, not some vampire." I pointed out.

"It was broad daylight. I stepped in. That's the duty," Aunt Dorothy said it like it was in the job manual and a given.

"I, ugh. I didn't sign up for this. Why now, why are they showing up? And I heard you talking to Brule. What did Lottie have to do with this? Is it why she's dead?"

Aunt Dorothy paused. I'd stopped her in her tracks with that question. I looked at the older ladies, and suddenly they were all quiet.

"That's not your concern. This town is your concern. None of it works without your generation of witches," Aunt Dorothy laid it out, there it was.

"Ha, I knew it," Tatum had been playing on the witch legends for years at the Frog Toe. It was good for business.

"But no more of that football voodoo. That's frivolous," Frances looked at Candy. She'd been very quiet for someone used to running meetings, but the football reference shook her out of her head.

"Glad you mentioned football. That vision at Lottie's coffin. I

saw very clearly that she had something to do with the bus crash."
Candy stood up. I remembered the list I'd found at Lottie's of the
football dads.

"That's awful, that's completely awful. I mean, we can make
small things happen, but if she killed them... I love having our
witch powers, but that's, uh, I hate her for that," Tatum was rarely
sentimental, but I could see her grief over losing Rick reappeared
like it was the first day.

"It is awful. She did it to increase her powers. That's it, isn't it?
I read about this when we started getting stronger. Lottie sacrificed people, oh my God, she sacrificed people to increase her
own power. That's how black magic works." Georgie had a
million books, and apparently, this was in one of them.

"Yes, that is how black magic works. A lot of us have power in
Widow's Bay, but here's a word to the wise: it shows up best
when three of us or more join forces." Aunt Dorothy looked just
as pained as Tatum about whatever Lottie had done.

"Did some sick combination of you help Lottie?"

"No, we wouldn't help Lottie. No one could help her," Francie
said.

"We've gotten stronger. I know we have," Candy admitting to
the supernatural was almost as strange as me doing it. We were
the two most grounded in the real world. I thought.

"Yep, nothing too incredible happens until you start pushing
forty," Maxine said.

"Can you imagine? If we had our full powers when our kids
were little? Sleeping spells, pee-pee in the potty spells? What a
cosmic waste that would be," Maxine said. I didn't have time to
unpack her sidebar.

"Bottom line here. Why did Lottie need, what did you call it?
Black magic?" I couldn't put the pieces together of a puzzle with
a blindfold on.

"She was keeping the gate closed. That's not allowed. That's
NOT ALLOWED!!!" Elsie was out of her head suddenly and

yelling. The conversation we were having was strange, tense, and surreal, but it was a conversation. We were talking, hashing things out.

But something snapped in Elsie. Her emotions tumbled out. She paced the room.

"Lottie has to be stopped. She has to." The woman had forgotten that Lottie was most assuredly stopped.

Elsie put a hand up to her forehead. She locked eyes with Aunt Dorothy. It seemed a brief second of connection, of clarity, and of farewell.

Elsie fell to the floor, Fawn and I rushed to break her fall.

The meeting came to an abrupt halt because it was immediately obvious that Elsie Faulkner was dead.

CHAPTER 17

$\mathcal{J}$ane Parrish had died the month before I returned to Widow's Bay, Lottie Bradbury the day I returned, and now Elsie Faulker was dead at our feet.

Three Distinguished Ladies of Widow's Bay gone in a very short time. Which left, by my count, three.

Frances, Maxine, and my Aunt Dorothy may not have mourned Lottie, but they were beside themselves over Elsie. I recognized their grief as something I would feel if any of my friends died.

And it stopped the debate. Tatum called 911, Fawn held the deceased woman's hand, and the rest of us stood in shock over the last few minutes.

"We're old, we're tired, and as you can see, dropping like flies. I understand you're confused and scared, but I don't have time for it now. I have to honor our Elsie. You can always text me if you have any questions," Aunt Dorothy said as the rescue squad took Elsie away.

We cared for Aunty Dorothy, Maxine, and Frances as much as they would let us. And we saw to it that the older women all made it to their respective homes. Aunt Dorothy was the least willing to take any help. The long evening turned into a long night.

But eventually, we all went our separate ways to digest, to rest, and to call it a night.

I'd had enough, but my friends were all more accepting. They were deeply rooted here, they'd stayed, they'd thrived. I left and bloomed somewhere else.

Did I really belong here now? I'd seen a lot, monsters even, but believing I had a part to play? That was something else.

I fell into my bed bone-tired, but my mind wouldn't shut off.

Had I summoned, that was the word, right? Had I summoned Brule every time the town broke out into a fight? How had I done it? Could I do it on purpose?

I sat up and decided between hot flashes, hormones, and hauntings that sleep was impossible.

My house pets were unencumbered by my concerns and slept like the dead in the lair they'd claimed, also known as the formal dining room.

I padded into the sitting room and looked out the window into the backyard. I remembered the dream I'd had, or maybe it was a vision.

A lock of my hair fell in front of my eyes. I brushed it back.

"Your face shines with all of their best."

"Whoa, what!" I felt like I jumped a foot in the air.

It was Brule. He'd crept into my house somehow. He came around to face me and sat on the window seat.

"How in the hell did you get in here?" My heart was beating out of my chest. Was this it? Was he going to bite the hell out of my neck? Did I believe he was who everyone said he was?

"You invited me in, remember?"

"That doesn't mean you can just waltz in here without a knock."

"Actually, it does. Don't worry, I know my way around this house. It's been in the family for generations."

"Yeah, about that? I'm supposed to believe now that you're actually Etienne Brule?"

"You already do believe it."

"I do not." I pulled my robe tight around me and tugged the knot at my waist. Brule watched every move I made. He was so handsome it was easy to forget the questions I had or even the healthy fear that should accompany an interview with a vampire.

"I knew many of your line, Nurses, Townes. You are like them, but also you are unique."

I wanted to find out so much more about the women he was talking about. My mother didn't talk about her mother, much less any farther back than that.

"They were all inquisitive, like you. But you're stronger. Independent. They were all very connected to their families."

"I was disconnected against my will." A memory of me explaining the divorce to my sons popped into my head. Trying to explain this current situation to them? Forget about it. *Hi kids, this my new friend, he's like 400 years old.*

"You're connected to me, me to you."

"Oh, please."

"I need you. There's no one else that can help me, what's the phrase, keep a lid, yes, keep a lid on all that's about to happen."

"What's about to happen?"

"Did your Aunt not explain?"

"She seems to think we, I, owe you some sort of debt."

"You do, I've kept many of your ancestors alive when disease, or violence, or even childbirth would have claimed them."

"Are you saying you made them, uh, vampires?" I hated the sound of that coming out of my mouth.

"No, but my blood does heal. And you owe a blood debt."

"What if I want to refinance?"

"Excuse me?"

"Whatever, forget it. I'm not getting into a deal with you."

"You're already able to summon me. That's all I need. For

now. We've only just begun to move back to these lands. More of us are on the way, and during the day, or when I'm otherwise occupied, I need you. You can keep me close. And I can keep any hostilities from hurting the town."

"Hostilities seem to break out left and right."

"Vampires and werewolves do not get along. They're always ruining the forests with their logging. We need the forests for cover and other things. Then, of course, the shifters, they hate the wolves and the trolls..."

"Uh, there's bad blood all over the place."

"Yes. It is my duty to ensure we all survive."

"And me? I'm your spy."

"No, you're my partner. I need you," Brule paused, and then added, "The town needs you."

The way he said need made my face flush hot.

"I haven't agreed to any of this. I may not even stay here. What do you think of that?"

"I can't imagine not seeing you now that I have," Brule said, and I swallowed hard. I had no doubt that there was something more happening between us, and I did not have a clue how to handle that.

"I'm a reporter. Okay? That's it." I squared my shoulders and stood in front of the Viking Vampire Frenchman Investor Home Invader.

"Did you kill Lottie Bradbury?"

"No."

"I'm supposed to believe you show up and then boom she dies with a hole in her neck, and you're not involved?"

"Well, ask your Aunt. We couldn't enter the county lands until she died."

"What?"

"Lottie was using powerful black magic to bar all of us from entering. It wasn't until she died that we could return."

Did I believe all this?

"Did you make one of The Crones do it?"

He stood up, and we were now an inch apart.

"The Crones? Well, now, no. I've found that I can't make you ladies of Widow's Bay do much of anything."

I didn't have a snappy answer for that. I looked into his steel-blue eyes, and for a moment, I was lost in them. I felt that connection that he said we had just as sure as if it was a string from my heart to his. If he had a heart? I didn't even know.

He placed his fingers under my chin and tilted it up.

Oh. My. God. I wanted him to kiss me!

He leaned down, and his lips were on mine, gently, slowly, and for only a few seconds, we kissed. It was enough to make me wonder about a lot more than whether he sucked blood. A vital piece of data if you're interested in pursuing a relationship. What's your stance on gluten? Do you like Monty Python? Do you suck blood to survive? You know, the basics.

A relationship? Uh, no. No.

I stepped back.

"See, we are connected. And I think more than any that came before you."

"I. You. Uh. I think you should go. Can I order you to go?"

"You can do whatever you want, Marzenna. But your destiny is right here with me."

"Do you always talk like that? I mean, really. I'm tired. I have to work tomorrow, and I'm not convinced you didn't suck the blood out of Lottie Bradbury."

"I will go, as you ask. We will trust each other."

"Right, sure."

"I'll see you very soon. And Marzenna, be careful. I did not kill Lottie Bradbury, which means whoever or whatever did, is still out there."

"Fine, yep, sure. G'night!"

"Good night Marzenna." And he was gone. I didn't walk him

to the foyer, he was just... poof, gone. I could not get used to that at all.

It was all completely disconcerting. He was powerfully handsome. He was also an ancient vampire. Did that mean mirrors, garlic, and crucifixes? Or sparkles? Were there different breeds of vampires?

I tried to unpack all he'd said. Questions upon questions piled up in my head.

Was I going to stay in Widow's Bay and be his early alert system?

And if he didn't kill Lottie, who did? I'd seen the werewolves. If it had been them, her house would have been a wreck, right? They were part animal. Nearly nothing was out of place at the crime scene but her larynx.

Brule said Lottie dying meant the door was open to him and his kind, but not before.

So, who else wanted that door open?

That answer led me right back to my own family tree.

My Aunt Dorothy had to be at the top of the list of suspects. I realized I had to confront her.

If anyone wanted Lottie dead, it was most likely someone who wanted the Yooper Naturals back in town. If I believed Stephen or Etienne Brule, which for some reason, I did, none of the monsters were in town until she died. That meant someone who was already here got rid of Lottie Bradbury.

It had to be one of the Distinguished Ladies of Widow's Bay.

CHAPTER 18

The next day, I sat at my desk at the Your U.P. News Office. It was Saturday, and the streets were packed with tourists shopping, eating at the local café's and generally livening up Widow's Bay for the All Souls Festival. Score again for Candy and Pauline.

The murder of Lottie Bradbury. That was concrete. That happened. It was either supernatural, or it wasn't, but the result was one-hundred percent real. She was dead, and no one was in custody.

Everything seemed so unreal in my life that this one thing, macabre as it was, grounded me.

I had a story, and it wasn't finished.

I ran over all the clues, such as they were. Lottie was killed in the middle of the night. Her body was discovered by the UPS guy. Those were the actual facts. Everything else was magic, and I couldn't write a story about that. I could barely believe that.

So, I went back to the old standbys: who didn't like Lottie, why, and who had the opportunity to kill her? Even more powerful, who benefited by her death?

The list of people who didn't like Lottie was long. But the list of people who benefited from her death seemed to grow every day as new residents of Chippewa County poured in and stirred things up.

If it was true that Lottie was the reason that the so-called Yooper Naturals weren't allowed in, a lot of people were impacted by her murder. And none of those could have had access to her to do the deed.

For Lottie to keep the gate closed, as they called it, to keep the Yooper Naturals out, because she hated them, she needed to kill. She required sacrifices; that's how black magic worked. I had no idea if that was possible, that she was killing to keep some invisible barrier up, but the list of football dads she'd hidden was real. I held it in my hands.

I decided to visit Loof. Maybe he could share something new about the investigation.

And I hadn't told him about the list I'd found.

It was Saturday, but the police were all putting in overtime to keep the peace during the All Souls Festival weekend.

I had uncovered an actual clue, and Loof needed to see it.

It was early, but Mary Jo was already at work.

I showed my i.d. because I knew she was a stickler.

I'd continued my research into Mary Jo since my last visit. I'd found out that Mary Jo had taken up Candy's old job as the president of the Football Boosters. I was going to keep working that.

I asked her about that first. If I stayed in this town, in this job, Mary Jo was someone who could help me with whatever crime happened in Widow's Bay.

"I heard you have to corral those freshman football moms, Mary Jo."

"Oh, yeah, at the meeting Wednesday, ugh well, these freshman moms. They're going to have to step it up." I noted the phrase step it up kept popping up in my life.

I understood the pressure to volunteer when your kids were

in school. Even if you did have a full-time job. I'd only recently left the mom life hamster wheel, and I could relate to Mary Jo.

It wasn't so long ago that I was knee-deep in working and mommying it up.

My baby birds didn't gently fly away to college. It was more like an explosion of feathers and then a sudden divorce. Even so, my football mom days weren't so far in the past. I knew that the minor dramas were major when you had a kid on a team. I listened to Mary Jo.

"Do you know they wanted SENIOR moms to put LOCKER SIGNS on the freshman team's lockers? I told them that this was NOT the way we do it." The pecking order was a thing, and moms who didn't follow it got pecked to death!

"You'll have to show them the way, sister. Hey, did that new helmet come in for Titus? Candy told me about that."

Mary Jo's son had grown so big that there wasn't a helmet in all of Chippewa County big enough for the boy, and the sixteen-year-old was still growing.

"It did. Coach said they had to make it special for him!"

"Wow, well, it's not easy keeping the moms and dads in line."

"Don't worry, I set them straight on that locker issue."

"Good oh, hey, I've got that recipe for Oreo Fluff dessert I mentioned. It feeds nearly a hundred if you need something new." I fished the recipe out of my bag and handed it to Mary Jo.

"Thank you," Mary Jo said.

"Can I go back? I need to check with Loof on that Bradbury thing."

"Oh, that reminds me! I heard Elsie Faulkner dropped dead at Lottie's showing?"

"Yes, The Crones are getting pretty old. This one looked like a stroke, though. Not a crime."

"Still, it's a shame. Jane, then Lottie, and now Elsie. That generation is just fading away."

"Yes, it looks like they are."

"I never thought I'd see the day without those ladies at every darn thing."

I needed to wrap this up now and get to Loof. "So, Loof?"

"Oh yes, sorry, go on back!" She unlocked the little half-door next to the counter, and I did just that.

I made a beeline for Loof's desk. He was finishing up a sausage McMuffin.

"Anything new on Lottie?" I'd used up all my small talk.

"No, nothing, sorry to tell ya."

"I have something for you." I produced the list of the names and handed it to him.

Loof wiped his hand on his pants and took the sheet.

"This is the directory for the team, what, two falls ago?"

"Yes, notice anything?"

"The crossed-out names?" Loof didn't need a master's degree in criminal justice to see that.

"They all died in the crash."

"So?"

"This was in Lottie's house. I found it after her nephew let me get pictures."

"Well, it's creepy, I guess."

"It looks to me like Lottie had a hit list or something." I realized how stupid that sounded after it came out of my mouth.

"Uh, okay, and she caused the wind and ice, so they all died? I mean, if she had a voodoo doll of the husbands, that would be something to consider."

Voodoo doll. Why did that click a switch in my brain? I brushed it aside, though, and moved on.

"Fine, I suppose it is ridiculous. I just wanted you to have the list."

"Is something wrong, Marzie?" Loof stopped chewing his breakfast for a second and looked at me a little more intently. Since I was already talking nutty theories, I proposed one more.

"Loof, do you think there's something odd about all the new

residents, the ones flooding into town for the logging and the ski lodge?"

"Other than them being vampires and shifters? They seem nice enough to me. Except, I will tell you a few were driving foreign cars, and you know that just doesn't fly in Michigan." I sat with my jaw open for a moment.

"You believe that stuff, the monsters, the witches?" I was surprised as heck.

"I believe it cause I've seen it. And I know you have too. Just don't turn me into a newt because I don't have a suspect yet in the Lottie Bradbury case." Loof laughed at his own joke.

"Aren't you worried that this, all this, is dangerous for Widow's Bay?"

"Well, Chief Marvin is, I just figure keeping the peace is my job no matter who or what's in town. If their snowmobile decibels get too high, I sight 'em. If they suck blood without consent, I arrest 'em. You get me?"

"I guess so. I'm just having a hard time adjusting."

"A lot of folks are in denial. There are some that see, and some don't."

Loof was unphased by the new neighbors. Loof taking this in stride helped me. I'd been wrapped up in angst and disbelief, and here was Byron DeLoof demonstrating a matter-of-fact attitude in the face of seismic shifts in Widow's Bay.

"And, you see it."

"Yes, and man, new money in town, that's a win. We had to cut three patrolmen last year because the budget was so tight. Now Chief is talking about adding new guys. It's good news, in my opinion. We've lived through the bust, and Widow's Bay is due for a boom. I mean this All Souls thing too; we're even talking new cruisers."

I nodded. And realized that had to be what a lot of people were thinking. The town was due for a good stretch, even if it did come with fangs attached.

I left Loof with no better understanding of who killed Lottie but surprisingly a better grip on how the town was handling the influx of magical population and mystical tourism.

Neighbors were neighbors, and if they didn't bite you and picked up their dog poo, things were generally going to be okay. At least in Loof's worldview, they would.

That helped me calm down too. And helped me focus on the most likely suspect in the murder story.

My own Aunt.

I did have a voodoo doll. A doll I'd forgotten about until Loof's off-handed mention.

And I had an inkling of who made it.

I fished the doll out of the back of my Jeep. I'd found it at the scene the first day in Widow's Bay.

This was no child's toy. This was precisely what Loof said, a voodoo doll.

Aunt Dorothy was planning to be at Elsie's place today to help with arrangements. I decided to head there next.

I was going to ask her a few questions whether she liked it or not.

I drove straight from the police station to Gray Estates.

I knocked on the door to Elsie's, and a familiar face answered. It wasn't my aunt.

Grady, the red wolf I'd met in the forest and at the cycling class, was there at the door.

"Uh, hi. What are you doing here?" I asked point-blank.

"I'm the muscle." Grady smiled at me, and I inadvertently smiled back.

"Yes, you do have muscles."

"Well, yeah, but I mean, I'm lifting boxes for your Aunt." He opened the door and let me in.

"That's nice. Did you know Elsie?"

"I didn't really, Jane and Lottie though, Elsie not as much. But your Aunt, when she calls, I come running." Where Brule conveyed an old-world courtliness that I attributed at first to his money and now to the fact that he may be a million years old, Grady was approachable. Easy on the eyes, yes, but easy to talk to, too.

"Is she here, my Aunt?"

"She'll be right back. She went to get a few boxes so we can be done."

"Ah, so you're part of the logging operation?"

"I am. We're almost ready to be open. Need a few more hands on deck, though."

"Can I do a story for the paper on that?"

"Sure, anytime, happy to help."

"Are you as old as Brule, however old he is?"

"Ha! I hope I don't look as old as that white-haired cadaver! No. I was born on this side of the twentieth century. But just barely." He gave me a wink, and I was struck again by his amber eyes. I was sure I'd never seen that color before.

"You're only one-hundred, a baby by comparison."

"We wolves don't live as long, but we do it better," Grady smiled.

"Do it better?"

"Live, of course, what did you think I was talking about?"

"No idea, lately I have no idea."

"And you know, just because you're The Liaison doesn't mean you can't have a drink with me. Liaison is a job, not a lifestyle. I'm a lifestyle." He was handsome in a different way, rugged, a little wild, but no less sexy than Brule. I shook that thought out of my head. Apparently, my hormones weren't done with me yet.

Just then, my Aunt returned.

"Grady, could you be a dear, the boxes?" She pointed out to her car.

"Yes, ma'am." I moved to the side so Grady could get by. He put a hand on my shoulder as he did, and I tried not to notice how my entire body from gray roots to pedicured toes reacted.

I had to put my sights back on where they belonged.

My Aunt and I were alone for a moment, at least.

"Aunt Dorothy, I want to show you something." I fished the doll out of my bag and practically shoved it in her face.

"Oh, my, where did you find that?" She looked alarmed, and clearly, the doll wasn't just a doll to her either.

"I am sure you know," I was guessing on that.

"At Lottie's?" Aunt Dorothy's brows knit together over her nose.

"Just outside on the walk."

"Oh, dear. I told her not to do it. I hoped we would find another way."

"Can you tell me what you're talking about?"

Dorothy took the doll and then walked over to a chair.

"As you've heard, Lottie was keeping the gate closed. She was doing anything to make sure they didn't come back."

"She killed the football dads, just like Candy saw at the funeral home."

Aunt Dorothy looked sad. And for the first time, old. I could believe that she and Lottie and the whole group of Distinguished Ladies were pushing 100. At that moment, Aunt Dorothy was ancient.

"It is so terrible. We were too late to stop her. I argued with her. Begged her. But she was determined to stop them from coming back. It was revenge for her."

"What revenge?"

"When they were here the last time, she fell in love. But her love, Carlisle, didn't save her brother. He was very mentally ill, they called it schizophrenia back then. Do they still?"

"Yes."

"Well, he heard voices, started fires, and it was terrible. He had a young wife and son! Then on top of that, he got physically sick with cancer. Lottie was so upset. She'd done everything for her family. And she begged Carlisle to turn her brother into a vampire. They can you know, turn people."

"And he didn't?"

"Carlisle warned her that it wouldn't really cure her brother, to be turned. And worse it could be dangerous for everyone. Can you imagine if an already unstable, violent person, becomes so powerful?"

"It sounds like a recipe for disaster."

"It is, and so her brother died. She vowed then not to help any of the Yooper Naturals ever again. And to keep them out. I just didn't realize how strong that vow was in her. She waited for decades, but she kept that vow. And she killed those men sure as we're sitting here to keep the gate closed."

"So, you killed her. However, you did it. With this doll."

"No. No. I thought I could. But I couldn't."

"Who made this doll?"

"Elsie. I ordered her not to use it, not to try to curse Lottie. I told her that if we used black magic, we'd be no better than Lottie. But I guess she didn't listen." Aunt Dorothy was softly crying now.

"But you wanted the Yoopers to come back. Why would you try to stop Elsie?"

"Honey, you're still not understanding. We're witches, yes, and we work with the Yoopers for the town, not against it. We're about community and family and protecting each other. And we can't be about that if we use black magic. The Yoopers are here, too, for that reason, so we all thrive."

"And Lottie couldn't see that?"

"Not after her brother died. She just thought they could have saved him and didn't. And she couldn't forgive."

"Why didn't you tell me that you suspected Elsie did it?"

"You've been having trouble believing things you've seen with your own eyes. I sure didn't think you'd believe in this." She looked at the voodoo doll, "Besides. I forbid Elsie to do it. I thought she'd listened. I really didn't believe she could do this to Lottie. But I guess she did."

"I guess she did."

How a voodoo doll worked to kill a person in real life was a Google search for another day. For now, it appeared that the mystery of Lottie's death was solved.

Even if no one was going to go to jail for it.

"Elsie, oh Elsie, I hope you're not paying with your soul for this." Aunt Dorothy was praying out loud now.

I put an arm around my aunt. I loved her, and she loved the town.

She ferociously protected it. I was in awe of that. Even if I couldn't follow in her footsteps.

I put my arm around her. I let her grieve.

At that moment, she was a woman who'd lost a friend, not a powerful witch that wanted me to step up and take her place.

CHAPTER 19

I helped Aunt Dorothy pack more of Elsie's things. Grady helpfully loaded them.

And then I saw her home. I was tired as I'd ever been and wondered if the end of Lottie's story would stay unwritten.

I couldn't very well turn in a news report about voodoo dolls and black magic.

But it looked like that's what happened.

Elsie had gone against Aunt Dorothy. She'd used black magic to stop black magic. I imagined a lot of people in the town would have been behind stopping old Lottie in any way they could. Especially if they believed, like the Distinguished Ladies did, like my friends did, that Lottie was responsible for the bus crash that left so many of them, widows.

I could imagine Joshua's reaction to me sending in a story to the Your U.P. News site where voodoo dolls and curses took center stage.

As far as the news was concerned, Lottie Bradbury's murder remained a mystery and probably always would. Random acts of violence can go unsolved, sometimes forever.

I came home and collapsed in the big chair in the sitting room.

Even Agnes didn't give me any grief. That's how I knew I must be a wreck. If Agnes was laying off me, I was a disaster.

She wasn't wrong. My head hurt after all I'd learned. I quickly dozed off, sitting up, with my mouth open until my phone startled me awake.

I was tempted to let it go to voicemail, but then I looked at the caller ID.

It was Sam, calling from his office at WXYD. I hadn't had a conversation with my ex since we signed the papers. And I didn't really want to.

But we were parents. It could be anything. I picked it up.

"Marzie, how are you? It's been so long."

"Uh, fine." He was cheerful and chipper. Like he was welcoming viewers to the show or something.

"I'm here on speaker with Alan, and he has an offer for you." It was strange as hell hearing Sam's voice, and at the same time, it was almost as familiar as my own.

"Hi, Marzie! Yes, we want you back," Alan Davis had only been the station manager for a year. He had presided over my quick termination during the meltdown damage control. Maybe if it had been Bert Zane, the old boss who hired me, I might have survived. But the new guy? He fired me so fast it made a sonic boom.

And I think he just said he wanted me back.

"What?" I was floored. I put a finger in my ear to be sure I was hearing what I was hearing.

"Yes, back in your old job, six and eleven, and a dedicated photographer for you for your investigative pieces."

"Excuse me? What's changed?" I had closed the door so completely on my old job so quickly that this felt like they were inviting me to be a space shuttle astronaut.

"We need your journalistic chops, and we were too hasty in cutting ties. That's our fault," Alan said.

"Damn right it was," The person who would smile through a job interview and hope for the best was gone. I'd lost her the minute I'd realized Sam was making a fool of me. I wasn't about to make this easy for Alan or Sam.

"And we're so sorry about that. We've done a lot of evaluating the future of WXYD. We're really committed to placing you front and center to help us lead the market. We were premature, that's become clear."

"That's right, Marzie, it's a great offer. I know we can do this together. We're mature. Our relationship has evolved." Sam was clearly talking out of his rear end.

And they were saying things now that I'd wished I'd heard about a year ago.

I decided the quickest way to end the conversation or see if they were serious was to lay out an outrageous salary demand.

"Double," I said.

I'd made a good living before, but it wasn't as good as some of the other big-name anchors in Detroit. If they wanted me, they could pay through the nose. I knew they wouldn't pay through the nose.

"Double the salary? Sure, yes. I think we can swing that." Alan said, and I was floored. How could this be?

"But we need you back before the end of the book, next week if we could, while November sweeps is still in full swing." The book or the rating period was the month of November. It was already a few days into sweeps, and they wanted me there before it was over?

"I can't possibly answer you right now. I need to think."

"The clock is ticking. I can manage the salary, but I don't have all the time in the world. There are other candidates, big names, that we're going to need to snag if you're a no. We hear Diane Williams out of Toledo is available. So that means the offer's good until Monday, end of business." Here was the hardball side of Alan Davis.

"I'm not a candidate, you called me. But I will call you Monday." A shut door was now swinging wide open. I needed at least a day to decide if this was right for me. Certainly, witchcraft and black magic were not.

I could barely process all that I'd learned here since coming home. Maybe this was the universe telling me exactly where I belonged.

"Thank you! And Marzie, we've missed you." Alan was now kissing my ass. There had to be more to this story than what they were telling me. And to have Sam make the approach? What? Was there a gun to his head?

I hung up and decided a call to Wyatt, my old producer, was in order. I knew I wasn't going to get a straight answer from Sam or Alan. I dialed the number at his desk in the newsroom.

"I thought you might call."

"So, you know?"

"I know, did you say yes?"

"Not yet, but what's going on?"

Wyatt and I may have fought over the years, but they were honest fights about what stories to cover, what should lead the news, and what viewers cared about.

He'd mostly stayed out of the hair, makeup, and consultant crap that I had to deal with. I respected him, and he respected me. Well, until I'd lost my cool on the air.

"This town is not happy with Sam. Our ratings are taking a beating, and you don't even want to know what the viewers are saying on social media about the home wrecker."

"No one thought of that before they fired me?"

"If it helps you to decide, you'll be in the driver's seat. They want to put your name first, do a big campaign."

"Sam is on board with this?"

"If he wants to keep his job."

"Wow, I'm sort of blown away."

"Marzie, accept my apology too. I should have gone to bat for you harder. You're the glue around here."

"Thanks, Wyatt, that means a lot."

"I mean, you're doing good stuff for UP Your News, but come on snowmobile robberies?" Wyatt chuckled, but I found I felt defensive. That was good work. And important right here in Widow's Bay.

"Hey, that was a good story."

"I know, I'm teasing you. So, what do you say?"

"I say it sounds like an offer I can't refuse. But do me a favor and don't let them know we talked. I told them I'd call Monday, take the weekend to think. I'd like them to twist in the wind. They deserve a little fear. Got it?"

"Fair enough. And Marzie, you won't regret it."

"Thanks, Wyatt." We hung up.

They wanted me back at the television station.

I'd have to work with Sam, that wasn't ideal, but I'd be in the driver's seat. And it was a job I knew. Ever since I'd stepped foot into Widow's Bay, the ground had seemed uneven.

Every step here was one into the unknown, and it was unsettling.

I was supposed to be in the prime of my career. I was supposed to be at the top of my game. Instead, I was here trying to navigate between myths and magic. In Detroit, I knew where I stood. And it was a good place to stand.

As much as I loved my friends, the decision came fast and easy. It was one I'd made before, and I had two beautiful sons and a major career because of it.

I was going to leave Widow's Bay behind again.

I wasn't cut out to be a part of this town's strange history. I didn't want the pressure of being what, The Liaison? I mean, really. It wasn't a question.

I would return to my old job, but this time I'd be in control.

I'd be on top and Sam, well, I wouldn't have to worry if he was cheating. If he was, it wasn't on me anymore.

I took a deep breath.

I looked around the old family house.

I was a bit wistful about not getting to fix this place up, but it was a house, and I'd left it before.

I crawled into bed and fell asleep.

Visions of French Trappers, witches, and werewolves floated in and out of my dreams.

As usual, sleep was a relative term.

I woke up Saturday and vowed to spend the day at home.

If I was taking this offer, I needed to pack.

I didn't want to hear or see anyone or anything, except my family. My Detroit family. I needed some non-magical interaction.

I texted the boys, and they called me to check-in. They were about to head out to Spartan Stadium to watch the home football game.

"I mean it's Indiana, should be a cakewalk," Joe said, and Sam agreed.

"I wondered what you guys would think if I took my old job back?" I thought I'd run the idea by them.

"They offered it to you?" Sam asked.

"Yep, I'm probably going to say yes."

"Bummer," Joe chimed in.

"Why, bummer?"

"Because I thought we'd be visiting up north this winter break. That ski slope sounds sick," Joe said.

"Not because you want to see me? Or poor Bubba!" I teased them.

"Whatever you want, mom," Sam said, "but they treated you like crap there. I'd say eff off if I were you."

"Thanks, boys. I wanted your opinions now that you're quasi-adults."

"Quasi-adult? Sam went to the bank last week, the actual bank, not just the ATM. I'd say we're totally adulting." Joe made me smile, they both always did.

"Wow! Next stop middle age!"

"Whoa, don't get too excited. We're not wearing Dockers or complaining about the thermostat yet. Baby steps."

"Right, I love you guys. Have fun at the game. Go Green!"

"Go White!" They said in unison.

Talking to them was good. I was also a little surprised that they knew about the Samhain Slopes. Maybe I would get a few more visits if I stayed. It was something to consider.

I puttered around the house. I'd been here for one week. I'd unpacked only a very little bit. It wouldn't take much to load it all into the Jeep. I guess that was a good thing.

The sun was about to set, and I knew I couldn't stay in the house any longer.

I had one more assignment for Your U.P. News. I had promised Justin that I'd get some footage of the All Souls Fest Parade.

It was the big finale of the weekend. Georgie said she would save me a parking space behind The Broken Spine and thank goodness. Downtown was packed again. The sun was setting, and the tourists were lining Main Street.

Georgie greeted me with a hug and Fawn with a Thermos of hot chocolate.

The three of us, my oldest friends, had plans to watch the brand new All Souls Parade unfold in front of us. We stood, leaning on Georgie's storefront as the sound of a drum cadence filled the air. We heard them before we could see them. A fire glowed from every corner. Little bonfires had been ignited in regular intervals to warm parade viewers. They added to the already magnificent pagan look to the downtown decoration. I noticed more garland and wreaths had been added. None of it was tinsel or Christmassy. Instead, it looked like a fairy garden come to life in Widow's Bay.

The new visitors to Widow's Bay were swaying to the beat, enjoying the scenery, and having a great time.

Mary Jo walked by and hugged Georgie and Fawn hello. Chet Gerwick, Shelly Prater, and a few others I'd interviewed for the Lottie story greeted me with a warm wave.

I felt accepted by the locals, my old classmates, and neighbors. I was surprised by how it made me feel. Georgie and Fawn didn't press me on any of the pressing issues that we all faced. We just enjoyed the floats as they made their way down Main Street.

Candy sat on the back of a Mustang Convertible with her campaign sign adorning the doors. Ridge was a few cars back but did the same. He may have hated the idea of the All Souls Festival, but he sure didn't hate the idea of using Candy's brainchild to reach a ton of voters. I hoped they remembered who made all this happen when they went to the polls.

Candy deserved to lead the town. She already had been.

There was a lovely tribute float to the football dads. A bunch of the sons and daughters were on that one. I watched to see my two friends let the tears flow a little as their sons waved at them. It had been two years, and a lot of healing had gone on, but still, it changed the course of the town forever. Had Lottie made it happen? If that was really true, a part of me was glad, she got what she deserved.

The grand finale of the parade was a magnificent float that looked like an ancient ship.

"What the heck is that?" I asked Georgie.

"Replica of the SS Bannockburn," she said.

It was that ghost ship, the legendary Flying Dutchmen of the Great Lakes. It was huge and had to be nearly as big as the actual ship. As a grand finale for a small-town parade, this was epic. Except it wasn't quite the finale.

After the ship, there were women, thirteen, some I recognized, some I didn't. They all wore white fur capes with hoods. They were young and old, but they walked in two lines of six and six. The 13th woman bringing up the rear.

The drums from the local high school continued. But there was melody on top of the drumbeat coming from the ladies in the hoods.

They were singing a song I'd heard before. I couldn't quite remember where. The tourists along the parade route got quiet, and it felt like everyone on Main leaned in to listen to the song.

I didn't know the words, and if it was English, it wasn't an English I recognized.

But the melody blared like a coronet from the women.

They passed by, and the parade, which was festive, turned into something extra. It was November. There shouldn't be fireflies, but hundreds of sparkly lights wove in and around the women who walked slowly to the beat of the cadence. Their voices soared, and it was almost a mass sort of trance we experienced. Georgie and Fawn held on to my hands on both sides.

The processional of women was nearly past us. Our eyes were on all of them while their eyes were facing forward. The harmonies were haunting and uplifting at the same time. I recalled the women and the ritual I'd dreamed of only one week ago. This was the song they were singing. It was a song that my Aunt Dorothy rocked me to sleep with when I was a child.

I knew the words and the melody, but I'd forgotten it. Until this moment when it reverberated down into my bones.

The 13th woman at the tip of the parade of women turned to look in our direction.

It was Aunt Dorothy, as she once was, and as she was today, young and ancient, in one time-shifting package. She didn't miss a note, but she nodded to the three of us.

We nodded back, and they continued their slow march forward.

The crowd began to clap and cheer for the parade, the topper for a weekend of skiing, food, and a touch of magic in Widow's Bay.

"We all saw that, right?" I asked Georgie and Fawn.

"Yep, your Aunt Dorothy isn't messing around, that's full-on Witch Guilt Trip," Georgie said.

"It was magic, and you both know it," Fawn said.

I didn't say anymore. It was amazing and overwhelming and more responsibility than I wanted.

Widow's Bay had a pull, and I was caught up in it.

I just didn't know if I wanted to be.

CHAPTER 20

I collapsed into my bed at home Sunday night, wondering if I could take any more magic, murder, or menopause. And amazingly, I fell asleep.

I must have dozed completely off at one point because a knock at the door jolted me awake.

Aaack!

It was almost nine a.m. on Monday morning. I never slept this late. I took that as a sign that I'd made the right decision to bolt.

I grabbed my robe and walked to the door.

It was the UPS man.

"Good morning, ma'am. I hope I didn't wake you." I figured my hair was standing straight up at this point.

"Oh, no, it's fine." He handed me a package. It was the silk pillowcase I'd ordered to eliminated sheet marks on my aging face.

I signed for it and then looked down. Something about his shoes caught my eye.

"Uh, are you the main UPS guy for Widow's Bay?"

"Yep, the town's got one, and I'm it." He smiled and nodded.

"So, you found Lottie Bradbury?" I asked him, and his smile faded.

"Oh, yeah, that was something. I knocked and knocked. She always answered, but this time she didn't. I knew something was up. I pushed the door a little and boom it opened. I saw her feet, you know, from the hall and thought she'd probably had a heart attack or something. Then I saw her neck, the worst thing I've ever seen."

"Very." I looked down at his shoes again. He wasn't wearing the standard-issue Rockport work boots, the kind that had left the prints at Lottie's. Instead, he had on running shoes, they were bright neon green with yellow accents.

"You always wear those shoes? Not boots?"

"Yep. I wear these as long as I can. The boss doesn't mind as long as I get the packages out on time. I run ultramarathons, the best way to break in my shoes is running up to the door."

"Did you look in the window at Lottie's?"

He shook his head like I was asking if the sky was orange.

"Nope. No time for gawking! I have a tight schedule."

"So, you just knocked, that's how you found her."

"Yep, and nice to meet you, ma'am but, that schedule. I need most of the town delivered by noon to stay on target."

"Sure, sure, no problem. Thanks for the package and the info."

"Sorry about Ms. Bradbury. She was always in a bad mood, but she also always tipped me at Christmas!" The smile returned, and he ran out, in his fancy running shoes, to his vehicle.

My mind was racing.

I scrolled through my phone. I'd taken pictures from the scene on the day of the murder. Aha! There they were, the footprints. Loof said they were from the UPS guy, that the man had knocked, didn't get an answer, and then walked in to find Lottie's body.

No one paid much attention to the footprints because they assumed the prints were from the UPS delivery man. He'd been interviewed on the scene like he said, and the boot prints didn't really stand out. Most UPS guys wore boots just like this.

Except for the UPS guy who delivered to Widow's Bay.

It was a small detail; the delivery guy didn't look in Lottie's window.

But it was a big detail.

I couldn't help it. Something in me had to find the answer to who'd killed Lottie, and maybe I'd just figured out something. I wasn't sure what. I thought it was Elsie's magic, but maybe it wasn't?

I got dressed as fast as I could, grabbed the picture I'd taken from Lottie's house, and drove to her place on Birch. The scene of the crime.

I drove up, and of course, the footprints in the yard were long gone. But that was okay. I still had that on my phone. I wondered if Kyle Bradbury was home.

I knocked. It took a few minutes, but Kyle answered the door.

"Hi, I came to return your photos and just check-in." Maybe going inside would bring me some clarity or some new clue.

"Oh, uh, hi, you're the reporter lady, right?"

"Right."

"Sure, come on in." The place was a mess. Lottie's fastidiousness was now a week removed from this home. And it looked like the nephew didn't care at all what it looked like.

"Can I put these back in the frames?"

"Sure, uh, in her room, right?"

"Yes, I'll be out of your way fast. I promise."

"No problem. Make yourself at home. I'm nuking some Bagel Bites."

"Don't let me interrupt."

I walked back towards her room and passed a pile of Kyle's gear.

I froze. Boots, a snowmobile helmet, and a Carhartt jumper.

I kneeled down and turned the boot over. I felt a spike of

anxiety, almost like a chemical, shoot from my heart to my stomach.

The tracks outside were from Kyle.

I told myself that it didn't mean he killed his Aunt.

I snapped a picture. And then I stared at the snowmobile helmet. It, too, seemed familiar. I moved on to Lottie's room, and pieces were falling into place.

"What are you doing?" Kyle had crept up behind me.

"Uh, your boots, they look sturdy. Good for all-weather, eh?" I was making completely idiotic small talk.

"Yeah?"

I decided to just ask. I was letting my inner Nancy Drew get the best of me. I had every reason to believe Elsie's weird voodoo killed Lottie. Aunt Dorothy believed it, my friends believed it, even Loof led me to think some things couldn't be explained in Widow's Bay, and you had to accept it.

"Kyle, these prints were the ones outside the morning your Aunt died." I showed him my phone.

"Must have someone around here with the same boots. Not a biggie." Kyle's eyes darted around. I started to realize just exactly what had happened to Lottie. And magic or monsters had nothing to do with it.

Money did.

"True!" I snatched my phone back.

I needed out of here fast. I was going to head straight to Loof and show him this evidence. Voodoo may be ethereal, but boot tracks were concrete.

Kyle blocked my way.

"The bedroom's that way." He pointed to Lottie's room.

"Here, why don't I just give them to you, and you can put them back?"

"Why don't you just give me your phone?" And then without warning, Kyle hit my jaw with the back of his hand. I felt the pain down to my feet and a coppery taste of blood in my mouth. I had never been hit like that and didn't have some fancy countermove.

I grabbed at the wall to keep me from crashing to the floor. I struggled to stand up, but then the little jerk kicked me in the ribs.

And then he yanked the phone from my hand as I staggered around, trying not to pass out.

"If you'd have left it alone, I would have left you alone."

"Kyle, you don't want to do this." He grabbed me by the back of my coat and shoved me into Lottie's room.

"Stay down." I crawled over to a corner and tried to get on top of the pain from the two blows he'd struck.

"Kyle, I'm sort of well-known, and if I'm missing, it won't be good for you."

"Don't care. I've got my aunt's money. Even more, after I sell this crappy house."

"You killed her for cash?"

"I needed it, she had it. She wasn't using it. And she was such a bitch to me. I always had to ask, prove I was clean, show her I had a job. She did the same shit to my mom. Like she was the queen or something."

I'd thought it was Aunt Dorothy or the Yooper Naturals, I thought Lottie's history with the town or her fight with the ladies was somehow to blame.

Instead, it was a deadbeat relative who killed her for cash.

"I have nothing to do with that. I can walk out of here, and we can forget you did this."

"Sorry, not happening."

I didn't have a play. There really was no reason for him to keep me alive. I knew he killed his aunt. It was just a matter of waiting for Kyle to decide what he was going to do to get rid of me.

I was scared. I wondered if it would hurt. I wondered where

he would drop me. I wondered who would find me. Or if anyone would find me.

I stopped my brain from continuing down that path. That wasn't going to save me. I looked around the room. Was there anything I could use as a weapon? Was there a way out?

I had no options. I couldn't get to my phone to send a message for help. And clearly, I wasn't a physical match for Kyle. He was young, and a drug addict or not, he was stronger than me.

Message. I could send a message. Or at least I could try.

I remembered how I might have done it when Fawn and Aunt Dorothy found me in the woods. I manifested the words in my head, over and over, and as forcefully as I could without saying a word out loud.

Kyle had decided. He had a pillow and was walking toward me.

"This way, we don't have to clean up any blood. That was a real pain in my ass." I pressed my back against the wall.

I let out a scream, but he pushed the pillow over my face. I kicked as hard as I could, but I couldn't grab a breath. I scratched, but the pillow pressed down harder. I was panicked.

My mind screamed for help. I pictured Brule.

And then, I was nothing.

Everything was black.

I didn't know for how long.

I blinked. My head pounded, so did my ribs. But that was good. I wasn't dead if I was feeling pain, right?

I blinked my eyes and tried to focus.

I was in the back of an ambulance.

I coughed. There were flashing lights.

I struggled to sit up and strained to look out the back of the vehicle.

I was alive.

But someone wasn't.

I saw a yellow body bag on a stretcher being loaded into the county coroner's vehicle.

"She's awake!" An EMT appeared at my side. On my other side was a large, handsome, red-haired werewolf.

Grady.

"Can you tell us your name?"

"Marzie Nowak."

"And what day is it?"

"Monday, like the worst Monday ever."

Grady laughed at my answer as the EMT checked my pulse.

"You've probably got a massive headache." The EMT said, and it was true. I was just starting to be aware of a throbbing.

"She's going to be okay right?" Grady asked the EMT.

"She's lucky. Going to need x-rays for that rib, but yes, all in all, okay."

The EMT smiled at me, and I was feeling in the neighborhood of okay but also shaken to the core.

"Can you give us a minute, please?" It was a question that came out like a command. I had questions for Grady, and they couldn't wait.

"Certainly." The EMT jumped out.

"How did you get here?" I asked him. And he kneeled in close.

"Brule, he summoned me."

"Summoned you, right." I shook my head slowly, and the pounding got worse. It didn't take a doctor to know that it was the result of no oxygen for however long I had that pillow over my head.

"It's daylight, sunny too. Maybe if it were overcast, he'd be out, but not today. He'd be a French Fry, hehe, get it?"

"Yeah, got it. So, he texted you?"

"Ha, now you're the funny one! Seriously he still uses a land-line. No. Up here." He pointed to his temple. "You called for help, and he heard. He sent me."

"I really don't understand."

"I thought Dorothy explained it to you? Well, at any rate. Kyle paid for what he did to you and what he did to Lottie."

Kyle had murdered his Aunt. It was coming back in waves. And he'd used the money to go on a binge, most likely he was freshly high when he stole the snowmobile and crashed into the Holiday Gas. My two stories coming together in a neat, although painful, package. The helmet, that odd black and yellow helmet I'd seen on the surveillance video and then at Lottie's. It was the last thing that pulled it all together.

"What did you do to Kyle?"

"You don't need the details right now. You're pretty banged up. You need to get better beautiful." I did not feel beautiful, but I did feel lucky to be alive. Grady stood up and hit his head on the top of the ambulance.

"Careful," I said.

"Ha, yeah, you take that advice. And here's my cell number, in case you need me during the day and don't want to go through tall, white, and vampsome." Grady handed me a card.

"Sure, uh, thanks." He hopped out of the vehicle, and the EMT showed up again.

"We're going to take you in. We need to check on those ribs." I put a finger to my side and realized there was a sharp pain there too.

They closed the doors, and we were underway, with no siren or lights. That was good. I wasn't in danger anymore. Lights and sirens always meant urgent. I was injured but not critical.

I leaned back and wondered how I'd summoned Brule. I marveled that somehow, that had worked.

After a couple hours of tests in the hospital, I was in a room waiting to be sure I was allowed to go.

That's when Loof showed up.

"Hey there, Marzie, you are doing okay?"

"Feeling okay, under the circumstances."

"I just. I'm so sorry. We totally missed the nephew."

"Do you have my phone? I have pictures of the footprints. I think they match the ones outside. And the UPS guy he wears different shoes."

"Yep, I scrolled through your phone and saw. We missed it completely. I think I'm going to be paying with some desk duty."

"Oh, I'm sorry about that, Loof." I was sorry. I wished I'd come to get him instead of going to Lottie's, but I didn't realize what I knew until too late.

"Nah, I deserve it. It was good that Grady guy was going for his morning run and heard you yell."

"Yeah, that's good."

"Kyle had priors, but they were as a juvie, so sealed, nothing since then. And his alibi checked out, so we missed it."

"What was his alibi?"

"A girlfriend. We just got off the phone with her, she admitted to lying, said he threatened her. Though I bet, he promised her cash or a stash."

"Wow."

"Yeah, real nice guy. We also found where he scored the night he killed Lottie and stole the snowmobile. He was high as a kite when he crashed. Wow, I hope that shiner doesn't hurt as bad as it looks." I hadn't even looked at myself.

"It doesn't, my ribs hurt, but they say nothing's totally broken, just a hairline crack."

"Ouch. Well, I'll let you rest. Again, I'm so sorry." Loof nodded toward me and walked out.

I was free to leave the hospital. But getting my clothes back on was a slow and painful process.

I also realized I didn't have a car. And I didn't know who to call. Did they have Uber in Widow's Bay? No, I doubted that.

As I walked down the hall pondering my transportation issue, my problem was solved.

Fawn, Tatum, and Georgie rushed forward, and Aunt Dorothy was close behind them.

"Are you okay?" I put out my hands. The idea of a hug was frightening in my current state.

Fawn took one hand, and Tatum grabbed my bag.

"You should not be carrying this. What's in there, a bowling ball?" Fawn said.

My Aunt looked like she'd been crying.

"Oh, I just can't believe this. How awful. We could have lost you."

"I'm okay, Aunt Dorothy. I'm okay."

"Let's get out of here," Tatum said, and we slowly made our way out to the parking lot.

"I'll bring the car around."

They saw me home. Fawn made sure my housemates were fed and watered, and Tatum heated up food. Someone had retrieved my Jeep from Lottie's, and it too was where it should be.

Aunt Dorothy insisted I go straight to bed. I wished I had the strength to argue, but I didn't.

"I'm just so relieved that Grady got there in time. I just can't believe that Lottie's nephew did what he did. It's just terrible that her own family would do such a thing," Aunt Dorothy said.

"You really thought Elsie's curse did it somehow?"

"I did, I also feel terrible about that. I owe her spirit an apology. A major apology." My Aunt looked tired. And she looked worried.

"Aunt Dorothy, you've done enough here. I'm okay now. You need to rest as much as I do."

"I suppose. I'm so glad you're finally here. I promise this is going to be the best decision of your life." She smiled at me. I didn't want to tell her that I'd decided to leave. That I was going to take the job back in Detroit. Nearly getting killed made that decision seem even smarter.

"I'm not sure I can stay. I have an offer back in Detroit. My old station." Aunt Dorothy nodded and looked like she knew this already.

"You'll do the right thing, dear. Your family is here now. We need you. They don't." She patted me on the hand and pulled up the covers around me like I was a child.

I didn't argue with her. Maybe that would be later. For now, I knew what I was going to do, despite anything she might say.

"I'll get Tatum to drive me home."

She left with Tatum. Fawn and Georgie walked in and took a spot on both sides of me on the bed.

"That Grady, something going on there?" Georgie asked me.

"You're kidding, right?" The idea that I'd be looking to date about now seemed ridiculous.

"He's damned handsome. I have to say handsome is breaking out all over Widow's Bay." Fawn said, and she was right.

"True."

"You're not staying?" Georgie said, and they both looked to me for that answer.

"You guys seem to be handling this supernatural stuff way better than I am. Maybe you always did. Maybe I ran away from this town as soon as I could because it's more than I can take."

"Or maybe because you are afraid of your own power," Fawn said, and I couldn't argue with that.

"You have to do what's right for you. You know we're here for you whatever you decide," Georgie added.

It was true. Fawn, Tatum, Georgie, and even Pauline and Candy were my new little family, now that my kids and husband were so far away.

"I need to rest."

"We'll let you do just that. Tatum left food in your fridge," Fawn said, and my two friends quietly left.

They'd come when I needed them. It was as good for recovery as the Advil and chicken soup.

I was tired, but I had one more thing to do. It was still Monday, and I had a call to make. I dialed the station with the old landline phone next to my bed.

The receptionist answered the main phone number for WXYD.

"Hi Elaine, it's Marzie, can you put me through to Alan?"

"Right away."

The call was fast. I hung up and closed my eyes.

I drifted off, quickly, and with no strange dreams.

Sometime in the middle of the night, I woke.

I looked up and gasped. The intake of breath sent a pain shooting through my side.

Brule was there, in my room, staring.

"I got here as soon as dusk fell, but you were sleeping."

"Don't you ever knock?" I said and tried to remember what I was wearing. Oh yeah, a flimsy nightgown. Ugh.

"Can I heal your wounds?"

"Pardon me?"

He lifted the inside of his wrist as though it was a water bottle or something.

"If you drink, they will repair quickly," Brule said, like duh, that's how vampire blood works.

"No, I think I'll go the old-fashioned route of ice and pain meds."

"As you wish." He moved closer, and I tried not to squirm. Squirming would hurt my recently cracked ribs.

He reached out and touched the bruised side of my face. He winced as he looked at it.

"I must look like dog poo."

"No. It just pains me to think about what might have happened. We all should have detected that little verminous creature sooner. And you should not have confronted him alone."

"I had no idea what I was going into, or I wouldn't have done it. I don't think."

"You must be more careful."

"Right, I agree. So, you heard me?"

"I did. You called my name, and I summoned Grady. He was the closest."

"Is that how it works?"

"Not always, but as The Liaison, you have the fastest link to me when I am asleep. I can do many things to keep the town safe. To keep you safe."

"How do I have this link? Where did it come from?" Questions I'd been afraid to ask bubbled up now. Maybe it was the painkillers.

"It's in your blood. Your line is connected to me and has been for hundreds of years. It skips generations now and then, but in you, the connection is strong."

"Great." I didn't know if I wanted to ask any more questions or pretend none of this was real. I could convince myself it was another weird dream.

"Sleep now." He leaned down and kissed me on the lips. I kissed back. I couldn't help it. He was magnetic, mysterious, and yes, handsome as hell.

"I'm fine. You can go. Thanks for checking on me."

"I'm not going anywhere until the sun rises." He stood up, and I watched him sit in the chair in the corner.

Brule watched over me, and I slipped into sleep again.

It was the longest stretch of Unicorn Sleep I'd had in decades.

In the morning, he was gone.

CHAPTER 21

The next day, I avoided my friends, my Aunt, and even Agnes.

I didn't want anyone trying to change my mind. I begged off, telling them I was resting. They believed me.

I should have been resting, probably, but I had to get out of there.

I was going back to my old job and getting out of Widow's Bay.

It wasn't that I didn't love the people here. I did.

But witches, werewolves, vampires, and whatever else they were talking about? I couldn't deal with it. I couldn't wrap my head around it. Even though I'd counted on it to save my life. I didn't want to be in that position again.

I packed my Jeep, slowly, and since I hadn't unpacked much yet, it wasn't that big of a deal.

I took one quick look around the house. I'd sell it. That would be it.

I loaded my animals and quietly drove away.

I rolled through downtown.

All Souls Festival was over. The traffic was more or less back to its normal zero levels.

But I noticed there were more cars parked outside the shops. There were people shopping and others sitting in the cafes. It sure looked like things were turning around for Widow's Bay. I was glad for them.

I'd got just outside of town and realized I needed to fuel up. I had a long day of driving ahead of me.

The odds that anyone would stop me at Holiday Gas were lower than if I'd seen anyone in town.

I mostly didn't want Aunt Dorothy to know until I was across the bridge. I knew this would be a disappointment to her, but I had to think of me. Not some legacy or weird vow.

I gassed up the Jeep and paid at the pump.

I needed some snacks for the road, so I walked into Holiday Gas. Things looked pretty good considering a snowmobile had parked inside the store less than a week ago.

"Hey, news, lady! They told me you caught the man who ruined my store!" Seyed was behind the counter, and he had a big smile on his face.

"Yes, well, sort of."

"It is good. People must know that retribution comes to those who try to destroy Holiday Gas." He waved his fist in the air as though fuel stop was a sovereign nation that would defend its borders.

"Right, yep. That's what happened." I put cash on the counter for my bottle of water and a bag of almonds.

"No, no, it's on me. You helped catch the bad guy." He pushed my money back.

"That's not necessary."

"Your money is no good here."

"Thank you."

"Today only, though. I mean, I am running a business." He looked at the next customer in line and started ringing them up.

"Understood."

I walked back to my car and noticed the parking lot was bumper to bumper. People were waiting for pumps. I did wonder if Ridge Schutte was right to be at least a little concerned about the influx and outflow of people. It could be annoying.

As I made my way to my car, a pickup truck and panel van both tried to pull into the gas pump spot that had opened in front of me.

One vehicle came in from one direction and one from another.

"I was next!" A very hairy dude in the pickup said to the man driving the van. The man in the van was stocky, bald, and had a large gold earring dangling from his lobe.

"Like hell, you were. I was waiting there for the last ten minutes!" Neither vehicle moved. But the men did. The man with the earing got out, and in response, so did the man in the truck. I could see the van was filled with littler versions of the driver.

They spilled forward into the front seat as the bald man rushed the hairy pickup driver.

This was going south fast. I shot a message, this time on purpose, and without question. But no matter what I did, these two were about to come to blows in the parking lot. I couldn't wait for Brule and whatever method he would use to diffuse this situation.

There were families in minivans watching, other trucks were inching up on the van. In a hot second, the Holiday Gas could turn into a powder keg.

"Hey, hey! I'm leaving! Take my spot." I yelled, and both of the men looked at me.

I pointed to my spot.

"You pull in here with your truck, you can have this pump. Everybody's happy."

"Like the lady says, everyone's happy." And there was Grady

again, to the rescue as my backup. I had no idea where he'd come from, but there he was, staring at the two warring motorists.

"I was closest," he said to me under his breath.

"Uh-huh."

The two men who'd seconds ago looked like they were about to start World War Three inched back to their vehicles.

I looked at Grady.

"You're always the closest."

"Ha? Really. Just lucky, I guess." He walked me to my Jeep an opened my front door.

"Thanks."

"Looks like you're going on a trip, pets and all. Not leaving Widow's Bay, so soon are you?"

"Yeah, actually, better offer." I pushed the ignition button.

"Move it, lady! We don't have all day!" The man in the van was now gesturing at me.

"Give it a rest, Onas!" Grady yelled back.

"You know that guy?"

"Yeah, that troll, we go way back. This one time…"

"Uh, some other time. I'm holding up the line here."

"Right, right. I can't imagine an offer better than this place. It's damn near perfect. Onas excluded, of course." Grady said. I laughed and slowly pulled out of the spot. I waved him a quick goodbye.

I left the handsome red wolf standing alone at the Holiday Gas. I didn't want him to try to talk me out of it or summon something or someone. I really had no idea what anyone around here was truly capable of, including me.

I glanced in the rearview. The risk of a fight appeared over.

I drove a little farther, away from the traffic, away from Widow's Bay.

I looked over my shoulder again. The town was in the distance, and beyond that, I could see the water.

Samhain Slopes was now open for skiing, and the mountain framed the bay as I looked back at it.

Something made me stop. It really was gorgeous. I wanted one more look. Maybe I would never be back. I pulled to the side of the road.

In this entire week, I hadn't really stopped to look. I hadn't really appreciated how beautiful this place was.

Don't be a fool.

Agnes had been quiet as I'd packed us up.

"What?"

These people need you.

"Excuse me?"

Don't go backward.

"Mind your business, Agnes."

I put the Jeep in drive and eased back out onto the road.

But she was right. Sure, maybe they wanted me for ratings at WXYD, but here they wanted me for a lot more.

Maybe they even did need me.

I thought about how good it felt to be near my friends. How fast they came when I needed them.

And how much I didn't want to sit next to Sam and pretend to listen to him. I'd done that for far too long, for the kids, for my career, and for a paycheck. Did I want that again? This time the kids weren't a factor. They'd given me their blessing to do what I wanted.

Do what I wanted. That was another thing.

Did I want to go back to having consultants tell me how to talk, walk, and color my hair?

I enjoyed freedom working for Garrett DeWitt and Your U.P. News that I'd never experienced in twenty years of working for big media conglomerates.

They trusted my news judgment. They let me pursue the stories I wanted to cover. That was never true at WXYD.

From somewhere I heard the cadence of drums. It was like the parade.

And I swore I heard the song the ladies sang.

I looked around. I was alone but for the pets in my Jeep.

But the song was as distinct and real as the steering wheel in my hands.

I belonged in Widow's Bay.

It washed over me. I belonged in Widow's Bay.

This was my home once, and it was again now.

I was still afraid of the magic, the myths, and the monsters, no question.

But I was letting fear get in the way of an adventure. Maybe even the purpose of my life now that I didn't have little kids to raise.

In Widow's Bay, I'd discovered that I was a part of something weird, ancient, and magical. I had thought magic was something for the very young or very old.

I was wrong.

If this place was going to thrive, maybe, just maybe, I could help.

I didn't know if I was willing to be The Liaison or serve on some magical chamber of commerce around here. But I didn't want to leave. Not yet.

Almost leaving made me realize I was brave enough to stay. And my mind was open enough to admit, now, finally, that maybe these powers weren't a curse. Maybe they had a purpose?

I wanted to stay, and I didn't want to be the anchorwoman in Detroit anymore.

Detroit didn't need me. I mean, maybe the Lions Football franchise needed some magical intervention, but no witch was powerful enough to fix that mess. Unless there was an Aaron Rodgers voodoo doll somewhere.

I picked up my phone.

I was going to tell Your U.P. News that it wasn't working out during my long drive South. I was so glad I waited to make that call.

I'd never written up the final story on Lottie either since I'd become a part of it. I'd planned to let someone else deal with it as I snuck out of town.

Lottie's story, the stories of Widow's Bay, they were my stories to write. I speed-dialed the number.

"Hey Justin, wait until you hear who killed Lottie Bradbury? I've got the scoop."

"Awesome. I can't wait to read it. Do we need to push alert? Breaking news?"

"Give me one hour. Don't worry, no one has this but me."

"Sure. You're killing it. Garrett DeWitt says you get to do what you want. Quick, though, can you swing over to the Do It Yourself Hardware after you post the murder story? DNR's doing free snowmobile decibel checks. People love free."

"And cats. I'm on my way."

I did a U-Turn and pointed the Jeep in the direction of Widow's Bay.

"Don't say a word."

Yes, I was talking to my cat. Agnes rearranged herself on Bubba's hunches.

And mercifully for once, she didn't answer back.

THE END

COVEN MITT

Up Next - Coven Mitt
Widow's Bay Book Two

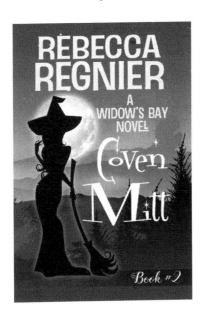

A Note From Rebecca

I hope you enjoyed *Resting Witch Face.* Consider leaving a review on Amazon. It's the best way for readers to discover new books and authors.

I get a lot of reader requests for **MORE AGNES,** and I have some great news. Agnes, the fashion-forward super snarky kitty, is the star of her own story. *Agnes Saves the Night* is free and exclusive to my newsletter subscribers. Just sign up for my newsletter, and I'll email you *Agnes Saves the Night.*

Thank You and see you back in Widow's Bay for Book Two - *Coven Mitt!*

Sincerely,

Rebecca Regnier

ABOUT THE AUTHOR

Rebecca Regnier is an award-winning newspaper columnist and former television news anchor. She lives in Michigan with her husband and sons.
rebeccaregnier.com

Made in the USA
Las Vegas, NV
11 October 2021